Charles Adams

# Poet Preacher

SALZWASSER VERLAG

## Charles Adams

# Poet Preacher

Reprint of the original, first published in 1859.

1st Edition 2023 | ISBN: 978-3-37514-163-9

Verlag (Publisher): Salzwasser Verlag GmbH, Zeilweg 44, 60439 Frankfurt, Deutschland
Vertretungsberechtigt (Authorized to represent): E. Roepke, Zeilweg 44, 60439 Frankfurt, Deutschland
Druck (Print): Books on Demand GmbH, In de Tarpen 42, 22848 Norderstedt, Deutschland

# POET PREACHER:

A Brief Memorial of

# CHARLES WESLEY,

THE EMINENT PREACHER AND POET.

By CHARLES ADAMS.

FIVE ILLUSTRATIONS.

New York:
PUBLISHED BY CARLTON & PORTER,
SUNDAY-SCHOOL UNION, 200 MULBERRY-STREET.

CHARLES WESLEY AND THE ARCHBISHOP.

# PREFACE.

THIS unpretending compilation is designed to supply a want in our Sabbath-school literature. It has seemed to me that a memorial of Charles Wesley, canvassing the main and important facts of his career, drawn up with appropriate brevity and sprightliness, and in a shape to attract youthful readers, would be of positive use to the Church.

The English biography by Jackson, which was republished at New York in 1842, and from which this little volume is principally compiled, has its value as a book for ministers, and for the study; but is quite too voluminous and cumbersome for common readers. In fact, the spirit of the age and the American taste require that authors who would be read must be brief, and earnest, and "to the point." They must be chary of side-issues, characters, and reflections; deal sparingly in generalities, keep the subject of their pencilings as vividly as possible before the eye, and cease their touches as soon as the picture is finished.

Such has been the endeavor in the little volume hereby submitted to the public. The story of Charles Wesley is highly instructive, and, for the most part, greatly beautiful; and it is hoped that the present version of it may not be unwelcome to the youth of the land.

THE EDITOR.

# CONTENTS.

# Illustrations.

# THE POET PREACHER.

## EARLY DAYS.

Charles Wesley was born December 18, 1708. He was the youngest son of Rev. Samuel Wesley, rector of Epworth, and five years younger than his brother, the celebrated John Wesley, the founder of Methodism.

His mother, Susanna Wesley, was a more than ordinary woman, being characterized by sincere piety, a strong and well cultivated mind, elevated views of parental duty and responsibility, and uncommon talent and energy as a Christian mother.

Under her tuition all her children were severally placed, and all were trained in accordance with the most careful rules of instruction and discipline. Never, perhaps, were children more blessed in a mother than Charles Wesley and his brothers and sisters; and never did children receive more faithful attention and care with a view to their growing up in true knowledge and wisdom. Nor can it be reasonably doubted that maternal influence upon the Wesleys had much to do with shaping their future character and destiny. "They were trained to habits of regularity, diligence, order, self-denial, honesty, benevolence, seriousness, and devotion, and well did they, by the grace of the Holy Spirit, reward the pious toil of their accomplished preceptress."

At eight years of age Charles was sent to Westminster School, and was placed under the care of his brother Samuel, then an usher in the establishment. Here he became an excellent classical scholar, while at the same time, under the influence of his brother, he imbibed strong High Church views.

While at Westminster Garret Wesley, Esq., a gentleman of large fortune, residing in Ireland, offered to adopt Charles and make him

WESTMINSTER SCHOOL.

his heir if he would leave England and reside with him in Ireland. But Charles declined the offer. "A fair escape!" wrote his brother John, in alluding to this circumstance.

Such are the pivots on which turn life's great destinies, and the destinies, too, of that great eternity to which we hasten.

It seemed a brilliant and captivating offer which was thus made to Charles, and the world would be inclined to pity him for declining it. Yet had he accepted it he would doubtless have walked another path from the one he actually traveled; lived for this world rather than for a better, and received his portion *here* rather than *there*. "There is a way that seemeth right unto a man, but the end thereof are the ways of death."

The sequel of the above-named matter was curious. Charles having declined the offer of Garret Wesley, the latter adopted a kinsman, on condition of his receiving the name of Wesley. This young man was afterward raised to the peerage, under the title of Baron Mornington, and was the grandfather of the great Duke of Wellington.

This case is finely summed up by Mr. Jackson as follows:

"Had Mr. Charles Wesley accepted the proposal that was made to him, he would have been far removed from the religious friends who were the instruments of his conversion and subsequent piety, and Richard Colley would never have possessed the property of Garret Wesley. According to all human calculation, therefore, the world would never have enjoyed the benefit of Charles Wesley's ministry; his incomparable hymns would never have been written; the extension of the British empire in India, under the administration of the Marquis Wellesley, might not have taken place; and the general who conquered Napoleon Bonaparte, and thus overthrew one of the greatest tyrannies that ever existed, might never have been born. What a thought, that events so immensely important, and involving the temporal and spiritual interests of millions, should have been contingent upon the volition of an impetuous boy, who was left to decide whether he would remain in England, with the prospects of poverty and labor before him, or go to Ireland to enjoy the luxuries and honor of wealth! That the hand of God was in the determination, none but an infidel can doubt. The youth decided under the secret guidance of Divine mercy, exercised not only toward him but toward the world."

## COLLEGE LIFE.

At eighteen years of age Charles passed from Westminster School to the University of Oxford. Here, though correct in his deportment and of highly agreeable manners and spirit, yet, for some months, he was far from being diligent in his studies. He improved, however, in this respect, but remained careless about his spiritual interests; and when his brother John, who had preceded him at Oxford, would sometimes address him on religious affairs, Charles would reply, "What! would you have me be a saint all at once?"

Yet after John had left the university to assist his father in the curacy of Wroote, Charles became much more serious, and apparently, too, without any special means being used for such a result. In this state of mind he writes to his brother as follows:

"God has thought fit (it may be to increase my weariness) to deny me at present your company and assistance. It is through him strengthening me, I trust to maintain my ground till we meet. And I hope that neither before nor after that time I shall relapse into my former state of insensibility. It is through your means, I firmly believe, that God will establish what he hath begun in me; and there is no one person I would so willingly have to be the instrument of good to me as you. It is owing, in great measure, to somebody's prayers, (my mother's most likely,) that I am come to think as I do; for I cannot tell, myself, how or when I awoke out of my lethargy, only that it was not long after you went away."

Nor was Charles alone in his seriousness. Being solicitous for the spiritual good of others as well as of himself, he soon succeeded in leading two or three other young men to become interested, like himself, for the salvation of their souls.

These thoughtful young men being conscientiously diligent and methodical in their pursuit of study, and in the improvement of their time generally, and being very regular withal in their attention to their religious duties, thus acquired the name of *Methodist*, and were known by this appellative all over the university.

Just about this time, 1729, John Wesley, at the earnest solicitation of a friend, resigned the curacy which he held under his father, and returned to Oxford. Charles and his companions were greatly rejoiced at his arrival, and they immediately formed themselves into a society under John's superintendence. The object of the association was to promote, in a manner more regular and systematic than ever, their intellectual, moral, and spiritual improvement.

will make the whole both pleasing and delightful to you. But for all that you must find time every day for walking, which you know you may do with advantage to your pupils; and a little more robust exercise, now and then, will do you no harm. You are now launched fairly, Charles. Hold up your head, and swim like a man; and when you cuff the wave beneath you, say to it, much as another hero did,

"*Carolum vehis, et Caroli fortunam.*"*

But always keep your eye fixed above the polar star; and so God send you a good voyage through the troublesome sea of life, which is the hearty prayer of your loving father."

---

## THE SOCIETY.

The little society of Methodists increased, though slowly. Several pupils became connected with it, and among others James Her-

* "Thou carriest Charles, and Charles's fortune."

vey, author of the "Meditations," and two or three years afterward, George Whitefield, who subsequently became so celebrated as a preacher of Christ. One or two extracts from Whitefield's correspondence at this time will interest the thoughtful.

He writes: "The young men, so called, were then much talked of at Oxford. I had heard of and loved them before I came to the university; and so strenuously defended them, when I heard them reviled by the students, that they began to think that I also in time should be one of them."

Receiving an invitation from Charles Wesley to breakfast with him, he writes: "I thankfully embraced the opportunity; and, blessed be God, it was one of the most profitable visits I ever made in my life. My soul, at the time, was athirst for some spiritual friends to lift up my hands when they hung down, and to strengthen my feeble knees. He soon discovered it, and, like a wise winner of souls, made all his discourses tend that way."

"God soon showed me," he adds, "that true religion was a union of the soul with God, and Christ formed within us."

The following extract presents a summary of the efforts of this college society for benefiting themselves and others:

"They carefully avoided all superfluity of personal expense, that they might have the more to give to the poor; they supported a number of destitute and neglected children at school; they instructed the ignorant, and reproved the wicked at all opportunities; and for this end went into the cottages and garrets of the poor, urging them to attend the public worship of God, and supplying them with Bibles, prayer books, the "Whole Duty of Man," and other religious publications; they regularly visited the prisoners in the common jail, for the purpose of prayer and religious instruction, Mr. John Wesley preaching to them every Sabbath; they assisted each other in their studies, and watched over each other's spiritual interests with affection and fidelity. At the same time they aimed at an elevated standard of holiness, feeling that they ought to be entirely devoted to God. That they might attain to this state they used frequent fasting, and availed themselves of all the means of grace, particularly the Lord's supper, which they attended every week, regardless of public opinion and example, and unmoved either by the laughter of the profane, or the scorn of infidelity. In going to the weekly sacrament at Christ Church, and in returning from that sacred service, they often had to make their way through a crowd of people who assembled for the purpose of treating them with insult and ridicule."

Ridicule and persecution are indeed no more than what might have been expected under the circumstances. It was an age of infidelity, and Christianity was regarded by multitudes as a fable. Hence the new society was censured and many reproaches fell upon those zealous young men; their pious efforts reflected discredit upon the less zealous clergy, and their conduct was condemned as presumptuous and irregular.

Under these circumstances the father of the Wesleys was applied to for counsel, as well as one or two other clergymen of age and experience. The father exhorted his sons and their associates to persevere in their benevolent efforts. "As to your designs and employments," he says, "what can I say less of them than *Valde probo?* ("I greatly approve,") and that I have the greatest reason to bless God that he has given me two sons together at Oxford, to whom he has given grace and courage to turn the war against the world and the devil, which is the best way to conquer them? . . . . My daily prayers are that God would keep you humble; and then I am sure that if you continue to 'suffer for righteousness sake,' though it be but in a low degree, 'the Spirit of glory and of God' shall, in some good measure, rest upon you.

"Be never weary in well-doing. Never look back, for you know the prize and the crown are before you; though I can scarce think so meanly as that you would be discouraged with 'the crackling of thorns under a pot.'

"Be not high-minded, but fear. Preserve an equal temper of mind under whatever treatment you meet with from a not very just or well-natured world.

"Bear no more sail than is necessary, but steer steady. The less you value yourselves for these unfashionable duties, (as there is no such thing as works of supererogation,) the more all good and wise men will value you, if they see your actions are of a piece; or, which is infinitely more, He by whom actions and intentions are weighed will both accept, esteem, and reward you."

Who may calculate the worth to a son of a pious and intelligent father! The influence of such a parent is next to omnipotent, not only to sway a child toward righteousness, but also to retain him there and stimulate and encourage him in the paths of good. "For I know him," said God of Abraham, "that he will command his children and his household after him, and they shall keep the way of the Lord to do justice and judgment."

It was not long after (1735) that this excellent father died. Charles was present, and also his brother John, to perform the last offices of kindness to the venerable parent, and to receive fresh spiritual strength from his dying words. His sky was cloudless as the sun of life hastened to its setting, and he was then far in the advance of his sons in spiritual understanding and experience. "The inward witness, son," he says to John, "the inward witness! This is the proof, the strongest proof of Christianity." The sons understood all this well in after time, though not now. "Ye shall know, if ye follow on to know the Lord."

Some of the expressions of this dying father startle us like the music of prophetic voices. "He oft," said Charles, "laid his hand upon my head," saying, "Be steady! The Christian faith will surely revive in this kingdom, you shall see it, though I shall not." To one of his sisters he said, "Do not be concerned at my death; God will then begin to manifest himself to my family."

And thus the good old man passed away to heaven; and the great "manifestation" came, and the family became greatly distinguished among the families of the earth, and the name of Wesley is written high on the registry of eternal fame.

---

## MISSION TO GEORGIA.

At about twenty-seven years of age Charles Wesley, accompanied by his brother John, embarked for Georgia, then a newly established colony. They arrived in the Savannah river on the 5th of February, 1736. After remaining together during a few weeks, the brothers separated, John remaining at Savannah, and Charles removing to Frederica in St Simon, an island of the coast some leagues further south. Here, Mr. Oglethorpe, governor of the colony, had established his residence, and Charles seems to have acted in the double capacity of missionary and the governor's private secretary.

Both of these missionary efforts of the Wesleys appear to have been failures, and neither of them were of very long continuance. The radical and main difficulty lay in the missionaries themselves. The truth is, neither of them had, as yet, become savingly acquainted with the great Christian scheme. They were deeply *religious*, as has been already sufficiently illustrated. They were earnest in prayer and devotion; they were zealous in good works; they were intent on being crucified to the world with its affections and lusts, and on working out their salvation. Under the influence of such instruction as that of Mr. Law, in his "Serious Call to a Holy Life," they had long labored for salvation and peace by the performance of good works, rather than by simple and naked faith in Christ. "According to their apprehensions, true holiness is attained principally by means of sufferings, mental and bodily; and hence they adopted this mode of life, resolved to do and suffer whatever it should please God to lay upon them. Their theological views were not only defective, but erroneous. They understood not the true nature of a sinner's justification before God; nor the faith by which it is obtained; nor its connection with sanctification. Holiness of heart and life was the object of their eager pursuit, and this they sought, not by *faith*, but by *works*, and personal austerity, according to the misleading doctrine of Mr. Law. 'Our end in leaving our native country,' says Mr. John Wesley, 'was not to avoid want, (God having given us plenty of temporal blessings,) nor to gain the dung and dross of riches or honor, but singly this—to save our souls, to live wholly to the glory of God.'"

Thus, of course, these sincere and zealous young men failed of the peace, the purity, and the joyous hope which spring from a full and lively faith in the atonement of Christ. In these great respects they were privileged to observe the difference between themselves and the humble Moravian believers who were with them in the same ship, on their voyage to settle themselves in the new colony. In the midst of an awful storm, when it appeared that the ship would founder in mid ocean, the two brothers watched the Moravian Christians and received instruction. "I had long before observed," says John, "the great seriousness of their behaviour. Of their humility they had given a continual proof, by performing those servile offices for the other passengers which none of the English would undertake; for which they desired and would receive no pay, saying it was good for their proud hearts, and their loving Saviour had done more for them. And every day had given them occasion of showing a meekness which no injury could move. If they were pushed, struck, or thrown down, they rose again and went away; but no complaint was found in their mouth. There was now an opportunity of trying whether they were delivered from the spirit of fear, as well as from that of pride, anger, and revenge. In the midst of the psalm wherewith their service began, the sea broke over, split the mainsail in pieces, covered the ship, and poured in between the decks, as if the great deep had already swallowed us up.

A terrible screaming began among the English. The Germans calmly sung on. I asked one of them afterward, 'Was you not afraid?'

"'I thank God, no.'

"I asked, 'But were not your women and children afraid?'

"He replied mildly, 'No; our women and children are not afraid to die.'"

But the voyage was finished, and Charles Wesley was at his mission in Frederica. There he was punctual, diligent, self-denying, and faithful. No Pharisee could be more exact as to outward observances. But, alas! "the glory that excelleth" was not there. The missionary preached, and his preaching reproved vice and sin with desperate severity; it held up the standard of holiness; it denounced vengeance upon all who came short of it. It was Sinai instead of Mount Zion. It was dark clouds intermingled with no genial sunshine.

The people of Frederica were unsettled. "They were under continual alarms from the Spaniards; many of them were without moral principle, regarded his ministry as an attack upon private character, and acted toward him as spies and informers, with little respect for either truth or probability; his health was not good; he was destitute of almost every personal accommodation, living in a hut, mostly lying upon the ground; conducting public worship some times in the open air, under the shade of a tree, and at other times in the place where the public stores were kept; while, at the same time, the governor was capricious, passionate, and under the influence of wicked people."

Such was Charles's unpleasant situation while at this mission. But it was happily of short continuance. He was soon called to Savannah, and after a few weeks, having resigned his secretaryship, he embarked for England.

## HOMEWARD VOYAGE.

The voyage was perilous and dreadful. Charles describes the captain as "the most beastly man I ever saw: a lewd, drunken, quarrelsome fool praying, yet swearing continually. The first sight I had of him was upon the cabin floor, stark naked and dead drunk."

Hence, but for the skill and fidelity of the mate, in all probability the ship and all its helpless inmates would have perished. In the midst of much peril, after a terrible storm, the pumps being choked, and the ship leaking badly, the following conversation took place between the captain and his mate:

*Mate.* Captain Indivine, what would you have us do? what course would you have us steer to-night?

*Captain.* Even what course you will; we have a fair wind.

*M.* Yes, sir; and it drives us full upon the land, which cannot be many leagues off.

*C.* Then, I think, you had better keep forward.

*M.* Would you have us go on all night and venture running upon the land?

*C.* I do'nt know. Go on.

*M.* But there are shoals and rocks before us.

*C.* Why, then, have a good look-out.

*M.* But you can't see twice the ship's length. What would you order me to do?

*C.* These rebels and emissaries have excited you to come to ask for orders; I don't know what you mean.

*M.* Sir, nobody has excited me; I come, as it is my duty, to my captain for directions.

*C.* Have you a mind to quarrel with me?

*M.* I have a mind to know what you will do.

*C.* Nay, what will you do, if you come to that?

*M.* Am I your captain, or you mine?

*C.* I am your captain, and will make you know it, Mr. Man. Do what I order you; for you must and shall.

*M.* Why, sir, you order me nothing.

*C.* You would not have me come on deck myself, sure?

*M.* If you did, I should not think it would be much amiss. Some captains would not have stirred off deck a moment in such a night as this. Here you lie, without so much as ever once looking out to see how things are.

*C.* Yes, I have been upon deck this very day.

*M.* But you have taken no account of anything, or given yourself the least trouble about the ship, for many days past.

*C.* It is all one for that. I know where we are exactly.

*M.* How far do you think we may be from land?

*C.* Why, just thirty-five leagues. I am sure of it.

*M.* How is that possible? you have taken no observation this fortnight; nor have we got one these four days.

*C.* No matter for that, I know we are safe.

*M.* Sir, the most skilful sailor alive cannot know it. Be pleased only to declare what you would have done. Shall we sail on? shall we lie by? shall we alter our course? shall we stand in or off?

He went on repeating such questions again and again; but as to giving an answer, the captain chose to be excused, till the mate, quite out of patience, having waited an hour to no purpose, left him; and the captain concluded with, "Jack, give me a dram."

The ship put into Boston, where Mr. Wesley sojourned about a month, waiting an opportunity to sail for England. He was ill during all his stay, yet he seems to have found sympathizing friends who ministered to his wants. He at length re-embarked in the same ship which had brought him from the South, the vessel having undergone repairs and shipped another captain. But the ship was doomed to encounter another terrific storm, and continual pumping could hardly keep her above water. "In this perilous hour," said Charles, "I rose and lay down by turns, but could remain in no posture long. I strove vehemently to pray, but in vain; I persisted in striving, yet still without effect. I prayed for power to pray, for faith in Jesus Christ, continually repeating his name till I felt the virtue of it at last, and knew that I abode under the shadow of the Almighty."

The storm passed, yet other storms succeeded, and much of the voyage was tempestuous and dismal. Yet the gales subsided at length, and sunny days and favoring breezes crowned the conclusion of the voyage; and on the 3d of December, 1736, the weary voyager set his foot again upon his native soil, and under the strong influence of grateful feeling kneeled upon the ground, and offered thanks to God for his preservation by land and water, and in pain and sickness.

His numerous friends received him with open arms, and almost as one who had been raised from the dead. His brother John presently followed him to England, and thus ended the mission of these two brothers to this country.

## RELIGIOUS STATE.

Thus Charles Wesley and his brother John are again at home. They had been abroad upon a foreign mission, while as yet neither of them seemed to have come into possession of that faith which justifies the soul, and which gives peace with God through our Lord Jesus Christ. The seventh chapter to the Romans pictured forth their spiritual experience, rather than the eighth. They had not, all this while, become freemen in Christ Jesus, and knew not what it was so to believe on him as to rejoice with joy unspeakable and full of glory. They were deeply religious, but theirs was rather a religion of *law* than of *Gospel.* They were striving for the "righteousness of the law," rather than for the "righteousness of God," the righteousness which is by faith of Jesus Christ unto all and upon all them that believe.

Thus, of course, they were in bondage, instead of rejoicing amid the freedom and the peace of the children of God.

It was in this state of mind that Charles, shortly after his arival from America, composed the following somber, yet beautiful poem, entitled, "Hymn for Midnight:"

"While midnight shades the earth o'erspread,
And vail the bosom of the deep,
Nature reclines her weary head,
And care respires, and sorrows sleep:
My soul still aims at nobler rest,
Aspiring to her Saviour's breast.

"Aid me, ye hovering spirits near,
Angels, and ministers of grace;
Who ever, while you guard us here,
Behold your heavenly Father's face!
Gently my raptured soul convey
To regions of eternal day.

"Fain would I leave this earth below,
Of pain and sin the dark abode;
Where shadowy joy, or solid woe,
Allures or tears me from my God;
Doubtful and insecure of bliss,
Since death alone confirms me his.

"Till then, to sorrow born, I sigh,
And gasp and languish after home;
Upward I send my streaming eye,
Expecting till the Bridegroom come:
Come quickly, Lord! thy own receive;
Now let me see thy face, and live.

"Absent from thee, my exiled soul
  Deep in a fleshly dungeon groans;
Around me clouds of darkness roll,
  And laboring silence speaks my moans:
Come quickly, Lord! thy face display,
And look my midnight into day.

"Error and sin and death are o'er,
  If thou reverse the creature's doom;
Sad Rachel weeps her loss no more
  If thou, the God, the Saviour, come:
Of thee possess'd, in thee we prove
The light, the life, the heaven of love."

The youthful reader will be careful to detect a cold and false theology lurking amid this elegant poetry. While it sings of a deliverance from sin and wretchedness, it discerns no other escape than through the doors of death. All is bondage here, and must be till the soul departs "to regions of eternal day." In after days, when his brother John had learned that *faith* is the substance of things hoped for, he substituted that mighty word for the word *death* in the third stanza, and thus rendered it as evangelical as it is beautiful.

Yet while the young man thus "walked in darkness," and was "under the law" rather than "under grace," he exhibited a religious zeal which might shame many who profess to have received a greater light. "When he traveled in stage-coaches he read pious books to his fellow-passengers, endeavored to convince all people that religion is an inward and divine principle, and that every one should make it his first and great concern. In private companies he pursued the same course, and often with the happiest results."

Various members of his own family also shared in his solicitude and faithfulness; and here, too, he was not unsuccessful.

It was about this time that Charles visited Rev. William Law for the purpose of receiving some special instruction from a teacher whom he had so long and so greatly revered. Indeed it might almost be said that upon the writings of William Law he had meditated day and night; and it was mainly through the influence of these same writings that both Charles and John Wesley had been so long and so sadly misguided in respect to the true way of salvation.

The interview was well, and was doubtless beneficial to Charles, though in a way he never anticipated.

Being introduced to Mr. Law, he beholds "a tall, thin, bony man, of a stern and forbidding countenance; sour and repulsive in his spirit and manner, resembling, in this respect, the religion which he taught."

Charles unfolds, in full, his spiritual state to Mr. Law.

*Mr. Law.* Renounce yourself and be not impatient.

*Charles.* With what comment shall I read the Scriptures?

*L.* None.

*C.* What do you think of one who dies unrenewed while endeavoring after it?

*L.* It concerns neither you to ask nor me to answer.

*C.* Shall I write once more to such a person?

*L.* No.

*C.* But I am persuaded it will do him good.

*L.* Sir, I have told you my opinion.

*C.* Shall I write to you?

*L.* Nothing I can either speak or write will do you any good.

Thus ended the interview; and the last gruff response of Mr. Law contained much more truth than falsehood. He was quite unqualified to give counsel, by pen or speech, to an inquirer after the way of life. His religion, like his name, was *Law:* he seems never to have understood the great scheme of the atonement, and "he set his pupils upon the hopeless task of attaining to holiness while they remained in a state of guilt, and while the regenerating Spirit was therefore uncommunicated."

## SEARCH FOR FAITH.

But a brighter day was rapidly approaching for Charles Wesley, and by the door of faith he was soon to enter into the rest of salvation.

In February, 1738, he made the acquaintance

of *Peter Bohler*, who had just been ordained by the Moravian bishop, Count Zinzendorf, as a missionary to Georgia. Mr. Böhler was a young man of deep and enlightened piety. He was also a man of sound learning, having been educated at the University of Jena.

Böhler arrived in England early in February, on his way to Georgia, and spent several months in London in studying the English language. He was also very active, during this interval, in efforts to do good. In this work he made the best use of his opportunities, and his labors were crowned with great success. "It was under his instruction, more than that of any other man, that the two Wesleys were made acquainted with the evangelical method of a sinner's justification before God, and deliverance from the power of his evil nature." In company with John Wesley, Böhler visited Oxford; and it was here that Charles first met him, and became his tutor in the English language.

Presently Charles is taken dangerously ill, and Böhler is summoned to visit him. "I asked him to pray for me," writes Charles. "He seemed unwilling at first, but beginning very faintly, he raised his voice by degrees, and prayed for my recovery with a strange confidence. Then he took me by the hand and calmly said, 'You will not die now.' He asked me, 'Do you hope to be saved?' 'Yes.' 'For what reason do you hope it?' 'Because I have used my best endeavors to serve God.' He shook his head and said no more. I thought him very uncharitable, saying in my heart, 'What! are not my endeavors a sufficient ground of hope? I have nothing else to trust to.'"

This sickness of Charles seems to have been a pleurisy, and came near proving fatal. In informing his brother John of his illness, he writes, in the language of Dr. South: "*I have been within the jaws of death, but he was not suffered to shut his mouth upon me.*"

As he began to recover, the following fine effusion, descriptive of his state of heart, dropped from his trembling pen;

"Peace, fluttering soul! the storm is o'er,
  Ended at last the doubtful strife;
Respiring now, the cause explore,
  That bound thee to a wretched life.

"When on the margin of the grave,
  Why did I doubt my Saviour's art?
Ah! why mistrust his will to save?
  What meant that faltering of my heart?

"'Twas not the searching pain within
  That filled my coward flesh with fear;
Nor conscience of uncancel'd sin;
  Nor sense of dissolution near.

"Of hope I felt no joyful ground,
  The fruit of righteousness alone;
Naked of Christ my soul I found,
  And started from a God unknown.

"Corrupt my will, nor half subdued,
  Could I his purer presence bear?
Unchanged, unhallow'd, unrenew'd,
  Could I before his face appear?

"Father of mercies, hear my call!
  Ere yet returns the fatal hour,
Repair my loss, retrieve my fall,
  And raise me by thy quick'ning power.

"My nature re-exchange for thine;
  Be thou my life, my hope, my gain;
Arm me in panoply divine,
  And death shall shake his dart in vain.

"When I thy promised Christ have seen,
And clasp'd him in my soul's embrace,
Possess'd of thy salvation, then—
Then let me, Lord, depart in peace!"

Until this sickness Charles appears to have fully cherished the purpose of returning to Georgia as a missionary; but his physicians forbade the undertaking. He returned to London, and immediately suffered a relapse of his terrible disease. He had been much averse to the doctrine of a full and present salvation by faith, as taught by Peter Böhler; but he was now led to review this important matter, and further conversations of Böhler led him to see, far more clearly than ever before, "the nature of that one true living faith whereby alone, through grace, we are saved."

From this time, and when prostrate on his bed of sickness, he earnestly sought for this faith. "*I have not now the faith of the Gospel*," was his solemn declaration and conviction, and he would not rest without it.

A few brief extracts from his private journal,

"will best portray the man in this momentous crisis of his history.

"May 12. I waked in the same blessed temper, hungry and thirsty after God. I began Isaiah, and seemed to see that to me were the promises made. I found myself more desirous, more assured I should believe. This day, and indeed my whole time, I spent in discoursing on faith, either with those that had it or those that sought it, in reading the Scriptures, and in prayer.

"May 13. I waked without Christ, yet still desirous of finding him. . . . At night I received much light and comfort from the Scriptures.

"May 17. To-day I first saw Luther on the Galatians. We began and found him nobly full of faith. My friend (Mr. Holland) in hearing him was so affected as to breathe out sighs and groans unutterable. . . . Who would believe that our Church had been founded upon this important article of justification by faith alone! . . . I labored, waited, and prayed to feel, "Who loved *me*, and gave himself for *me*."

"May 19. Mrs. Turner came, and told me I should not rise from that bed till I believed. I believed her saying, and asked, 'Has God then bestowed faith upon you?' 'Yes, he has.' 'Why, have you peace with God?' 'Yes, perfect peace,' 'And do you love Christ above all things?' 'I do; above all things incomparably.' 'Then, are you willing to die?' 'I am; and would be glad to die this moment; for I know all my sins are blotted out; the handwriting that was against me is taken out of the way, and nailed to the cross. He has saved me by his death; He has washed me with his blood; He has hid me in his wounds. I have peace in him, and rejoice with joy unspeakable and full of glory.'

"Her answers were so full, to these and to the most searching questions I could ask, that I had no doubt of her having received the atonement, and waited for it myself with a more assured hope. Feeling an anticipation of joy on her account, and thanking Christ as I could, I looked for him all night, with prayers, and sighs, and unceasing desires."

"Such," adds Mr. Jackson, "was the manner in which Mr. Charles Wesley waited upon God for that great change in his state and character, upon which he felt that his peace and safety both in time and eternity depended. He was humble, penitent, teachable, and persevering. He read the Holy Scriptures; studied the promises of God; was diligent in prayer, both social and private; and almost daily received the Lord's supper. In obedience to the divine direction, he continued asking, that he might receive; seeking, that he might find; knocking at the door of mercy, that it might be opened; laboring to believe in the Lord Jesus Christ, in the earnest hope that the Holy Spirit would impart the full power of faith, and then witness his adoption, and purify his heart."

## SUCCESS.

On Sunday morning, May 21, 1738, as Charles Wesley was praying on his sick bed, having pleaded the great promises, and endeavoring to rely upon them, he was composing himself to sleep.

At that moment a female voice spoke at the door of his chamber, and said: "In the name of Jesus of Nazareth, arise and believe, and thou shalt be healed of all thine infirmities."

The sick man lay wondering, and the words struck him to the heart, and he sighed deeply, and whispered to himself: "O that Christ would but speak thus to me!" His heart sank within him, and he hoped that it might be Christ indeed, and began tremblingly to say to himself, "I believe! I believe!"

It seems that the above message, which had so startled him, was uttered by the pious Mrs. Turner mentioned in the preceding chapter. She knew his condition, and his earnest strife after saving faith; yet feeling her own weakness, she shrank from approaching a scholar and a clergyman, and speaking to him face to face.

At the same time she appears to have had a deep and solemn conviction that she ought thus to address the afflicted penitent who was weeping and praying for pardon and peace, and she obeyed her convictions.

"I never," said Charles, "heard words uttered with like solemnity. I rose and looked into the Scriptures. The words that first presented were, 'And now, Lord, what is my hope? Truly, my hope is even in thee.' I then cast down my eye, and met: 'He hath put a new song in my mouth, even a thanksgiving unto our God. Many shall see it, and fear, and shall put their trust in the Lord.'

"Afterward I opened upon Isaiah xl, 1: 'Comfort ye, comfort ye my people, saith your God. Speak ye comfortably to Jerusalem, and cry unto her, that her warfare is accomplished, that hor iniquity is pardoned: for she hath received of the Lord's hand double for all her sins.'

"I now found myself at peace with God, and rejoiced in hope of loving Christ. My temper, for the rest of the day, was mistrust of my own great, but before unknown, weakness. I saw that by faith I stood; and the continual support of faith, which kept me from falling, though of myself I am ever sinking into sin. I went to bed still sensible of my own weakness, (I humbly hope to be more and more so,) yet confident of Christ's protection."

Thus did Charles Wesley, for the first time, believe with a heart unto righteousness. Yet his early faith was weak, and he held the Saviour "with a trembling hand." But as he prayed, conversed, and studied the Holy Scriptures, his confidence increased, and his evidence of the divine favor became increasingly distinct and vivid.

On the following Wednesday, May, 24, 1738, John Wesley obtained "the like precious faith." He, like Charles, had been earnestly searching for saving faith, and was greatly encouraged by Charles's happy experience.

At a meeting on the evening of the day alluded to, he was listening to some one reading Luther's "Preface to the Epistle to the Romans." "About a quarter before nine," he writes, "while he was describing the change which God works in the heart through faith in Christ, I felt my heart strangely warmed. I felt I did trust in Christ, Christ alone, for salvation; and an assurance was given me that he had taken away *my* sins, even *mine*, and saved *me* from the law of sin and death."

Thus in almost the same hour came forth these two brothers from the darkness and struggles of a merely legal religion, into the peaceful world of faith. They ceased to trust in good works for salvation and rest, and began to trust in Christ alone. "They saw with increasing clearness that the Christian faith, which is described in the Acts of the Apostles, and in the apostolic Epistles, is not mere assent to the general truth of the Gospel, nor a mere belief of it essential doctrines, but a personal trust in the sacrificial blood of the Son of God, exercised in a penitent state of heart, and productive both of peace of conscience, and of inward and outward holiness. This became the principal topic of their ministry; and while its truth was to them matter of personal consciousness, they saw it exemplified in the character of thousands of their spiritual children. It was, in fact, under God, the great secret of their power, both as preachers and writers. Under the divine sanction and blessing they received this truth, and were qualified to preach it to all men, out of the fullness of a heart purified by faith from its guilt and natural corruption."

As Charles Wesley emerged from his long darkness into God's marvelous light, he took his beautiful harp from the willows, and swept it in such strains as these:

"Where shall my wondering soul begin?
  How shall I all to heaven aspire?
A slave redeem'd from death and sin,
  A brand pluck'd from eternal fire,
How shall I equal triumph raise
Or sing my great Deliverer's praise?

"O how shall I the goodness tell,
 Father, which thou to me hast show'd?
That I, a child of wrath and hell,
 I should be call'd a child of God,
Should know, should feel my sins forgiven,
Bless'd with this antepast of heaven!

"Long my imprison'd spirit lay
 Fast bound in sin and nature's night;
Thine eye diffused a quick'ning ray;
 I woke; the dungeon flamed with light;
My chains fell off, my heart was free,
I rose, went forth, and follow'd thee.

"No condemnation now I dread;
 Jesus, and all in him, is mine!
Alive in him, my living Head,
 And clothed in righteousness divine,
Bold I approach th' eternal throne,
And claim the crown through Christ my own."

## EARLIEST RESULTS.

"The day," says Mr. Jackson, "on which Mr. Charles Wesley came to Christ, weary and heavy laden, and found rest to his soul, was unquestionably the most important period of his existence. He then felt that he passed from death unto life. His spiritual enjoyments now began, in all their richness and depth, and he entered upon a course of ministerial usefulness of which, up to this period, he had no conception."

It appears that his health now rapidly improved, so that in a few days he was able to go abroad. He dwelt much and deeply with the Scriptures, wherein he meditated day and night. He went from house to house, and ceased not daily to teach and preach Jesus Christ. "In private companies, where many resorted to him, he read the Scriptures, sang hymns, related his religious experience, and urged upon all the duty and privelege of an immediate application to Christ, in faith, for pardon, and peace, and holiness. Never did he forget the bright and joyous days which immediately followed his espousal to Christ; and every remembrance of them was refreshing to his heart."

Some specimens of these early exercises and efforts cannot fail to edify as well as interest thoughtful and pious hearts.

In a company of serious persons it was particularly asked in prayer that some one might receive the atonement. One gentleman found power to believe, and rose, telling Charles that his prayer was heard and answered in him, and all were full of joy and thanksgiving. A day or two afterward another received faith while Charles was praying, though he did not then confess it.

At the same time he speaks of Dr. Byrom, a poet, who received the doctrine of faith with wonderful readiness.

Then he makes an excursion to Blendon, and as he rides is full of delight, and seems moving and expatiating in a new heaven and a new earth. He and his traveling companion go praying, singing, and shouting, all the way.

He visits Rev. Mr. Piers, a minister of the Established Church, tells him his experience with great simplicity. The good man listens eagerly, makes no objection, and confesses it is what he never experienced. At length he is greatly moved—longs to find Christ. The next day they pray earnestly with and for him, while Mr. Piers struggles for the blessing of faith. Soon he believes, and is filled with joy unspeakable.

He visits the Delamottes, a wealthy and respectable family residing at Blendon, and comprising the father and mother, two daughters, Hetty and Betsy, and several sons. They are all religious, but have not learned the faith in Christ. He finds the daughters at home, and prays that salvation may come to the house immediately. Betsy soon hears a voice whispering to her, "Go thy way, thy sins are forgiven thee!" and is filled with joy unspeakable. Hetty strives earnestly, and Charles strives in her behalf, till at length, in singing, he observes her join with mingled fear and joy. Presently she declares that she could not but believe that Christ died for her, even for her.

The maid also, hearing him read how that "He hath made Christ to be sin for us, who knew no sin, that we might be made the righteousness of God in him," is filled with consolation, and believes that Christ died for her, and feels that her sins are forgiven.

A day or two afterward Jack Delamotte calls upon Charles, in London, and tells him that when he was at Blendon, and singing, one day, of Christ,

"Who for me, for me hath died,"

he found the words sink into his soul, and he could have sung them forever, and was full of delight and joy.

Charles feels much for William Delamotte, who is a student at Cambridge, and now on a visit home. He discourses with him on faith and free grace; William objects. They walk to church together, and Charles again tells him of the glad tidings of salvation. William is heavy and miserable. "We are justified freely by faith alone," is a saying he cannot receive. He calls on Charles the next day; tells him he had been writing against the doctrines of faith, but having written two sheets, he, in searching for texts, read, "Not by works of righteousness which we have done, but according to his mercy he saved us." And this spoiled all, and convinced him of his error.

They proceed to pray, and Charles pleads the promises for him with great earnestness. Three days after he recieves a note from William, telling him that God had heard his prayers. "O my friend!" he exclaims. "I am free indeed! I agonized some time between darkness and light; but God was greater than my heart, and burst the cloud, and broke down the partition wall, and opened to me the door of faith."

While Charles was praying for William Delamotte, as just related, a poor man, Heather by name, came in to talk with him.

*Heather.* I heard and liked your sermon on faith.

*Wesley.* Have you faith?

*H.* No.

*W.* Have you the forgiveness of sins?

*H.* No.

*W.* Can there be any good in you till you believe?

*H.* No.

*W.* But do you think that Christ cannot give you faith and forgiveness in this hour?

*H.* Yes; to be sure he can.

*W.* And do you believe his promise, that where two of his disciples shall agree upon earth as touching anything they shall ask of him, he will give it them?

*H.* I do.

*W.* Why, then, here is your minister, and I agree with him to ask faith for you.

*H.* Then I believe I shall receive it before I go out of this room.

To prayer they went; and rising and asking him whether he believed, he replied, "Yes, I do believe with all my heart. I believe Christ died for my sins; I know they are all forgiven. I desire only to love him. I would suffer anything for him; could lay down my life for him this moment."

Mrs. Delamotte proved a more obstinate case. At first she was civil. Charles preached faith in her hearing. The next day, he calls on her at her house. She falls abruptly upon the sermon for its false doctrine. Much dispute ensues. At length she starts up and runs out of the house, protesting she could not bear the conversation. After a time her daughter Betsy prevails upon her to return.

A week afterward Charles hears that Mrs. Delamotte is convinced of unbelief, and much ashamed of her treatment of him. Presently she sends for him, explains her conduct, hears him further concerning the faith in Christ, and is thoroughly convinced. At length she becomes completely humbled, and Charles continued instant in prayer and intercessions in her behalf.

Four days after the above interview with Mrs. Delamotte, he receives a letter from her son William, wherein were the following words concerning his mother:

"She continued agonizing all the evening. But how can I utter the sequel? The first object of her thoughts the next morning was Christ. She saw him approaching; and seeing, loved, believed, adored. Her prayers drew him still nearer, and everything she saw concurred to hasten the embrace of her Beloved. Thus she continued in the Spirit till four; when, reading in her closet, she received the kiss of reconciliation. Her own soul could not contain the joys attending it. She could not forbear imparting to her friends and neighbors that she had found the piece which she had lost."

Such is a specimen of the zeal and the success of Charles Wesley in his earliest efforts to awaken and promote the faith which brings a present salvation. It was an auspicious morning of the brilliant and glorious day that was to succeed.

## FURTHER DEVELOPMENTS.

It was now the autumn of 1738, and Charles Wesley "began to be about thirty years of age." Himself and his brother John had of late obtained the "precious faith" which saves from sin, and is the root of all true righteousness. John had been spending some months in Germany, on a visit to the Moravians, and had learned much from their goodly discipline and order, and from their deep and sound Scriptural experience.

On his return the two brothers began to cooperate with each other for the advancement of true religion. Their plan was to preach in such churches as were open to them, and hold "meetings for conversation, prayer, singing, mutual exhortations, and Scriptural exposition."

Up to this time Charles had always read his sermons from the pulpit. But he now began to exercise himself in extemporary speaking, and thus acquired a boldness and facility of speaking, and a self-command which surprised himself as well as others, and thus it was that he became at length one of the most fluent and impressive preachers of his age.

The influence of his preaching, as well as that of his brother, began now to be felt among the more openly profligate and wicked. Many of these were brought to repentance, the genuineness and sincerity of which were evinced by a reformed life.

But neither of the brothers had, at this time, the slightest intention of departing from the established order of the Church of which they were ministers. Hence, when unfavorable reports of their proceedings reached the ears of the higher officers of the Church, they lost no time in waiting upon these dignitaries, for the purpose of defending themselves, and also of soliciting episcopal advice and sanction. They conferred with the Bishop of London and the Archbishop of Canterbury, by both of whom they seem to have been treated, at first, with kindness.

But Charles's ardent spirit, and especially his doctrine of salvation by faith alone, gave great offense, and provoked much opposition. He preached at Bexley, in the church of the good Mr. Piers, already mentioned. A part of the congregation retire from the church while he is preaching, and the vicar is alarmed.

At the request of Mr. Stonehouse, vicar of Islington, Charles became his curate. But he met with the most determined opposition in the discharge of his clerical duties. The bishop had not given his sanction to the arrangement between the curate and the vicar, and this strengthened the opposition. The church-wardens would meet him in the vestry, before the commencement of divine service, and annoy him by asking to see the bishop's license to his curacy. At another time, and in the same place, they would proceed to revile him, telling him that he was full of the devil, and all others who thought with him. Having failed to drive him away by these means, they proceeded to greater extremes, and took their position at the foot of the pulpit stairs, so that when, after prayers, the preacher attempted to ascend the pulpit, they forcibly prevented him, regardless of the presence of the congregation, as well as of all decency. The matter was presented to the Bishop of London, who justified the church-wardens in their conduct.

Thus was Charles compelled to seek other fields for the exercise of his ministry than the pulpits of his Church. He was literally expelled by violence, and that violence received the sanction of the diocesan.

Similar treatment awaited his brother John. It soon transpired that for the most part, when he had preached in a church, he was notified, at the conclusion of the service, that he must occupy that pulpit no more.

Mr. Whitefield met the same fate. He had just returned from a missionary excursion to Georgia, and was making collections in behalf of an orphan asylum in that foreign land. Attempting to present his cause in Bristol, it was not long before he was excluded from every pulpit in that city connected with the Established Church.

What was the matter with these men? There were two difficulties. One was that they preached the offensive doctrine of salvation by faith alone; and the second was, that such multitudes flocked to hear the preaching that the pew-holders were subjected to serious inconvenience. So much heat and crowding were too irksome and vexatious to be borne!

But God had his eye upon all this, and he had his great and wise designs in permitting so disgraceful and wicked an outrage. We shall see forthwith the interpretation. Clergymen and church-wardens may lock up their pulpit doors against God's ministers, and bishops may uphold them in such conduct. Nevertheless, "the earth is the Lord's and the fullness thereof."

## FIELD PREACHING.

Field preaching was the result of excluding Whitefield and the Wesleys from the pulpits of the Established Church.

Whitefield led the van in this novel and great enterprise. John Wesley follows with equal steps. "I could at first scarcely reconcile myself," he says, "to this strange way of preaching in the fields, of which he set me an example

FIELD PREACHING

on Sunday. Having been all my life (till very lately) so tenacious of every point relating to decency and order, I should have thought the saving of souls almost a sin, if it had not been done in the church."

And Charles was not behind. A farmer wants him to preach in his field, and he complies. Then a Quaker presses him to preach in the street, and he preaches to about a thousand persons. The next day he preaches again, and many are moved under the word. Then he preaches in Moorfields to ten thousand people, and invites them to come to the Saviour and find rest. Presently he preaches at Kennington Common to "multitudes upon multitudes," calling upon them to "repent and believe the Gospel;" and he writes that the Lord was his "strength, and mouth, and wisdom." He continues preaching at Moorfields and Kennington Common to immense assemblies, and to the great joy and spiritual benefit of many.

He is at this time in labors more abundant, visiting prisoners, praying with penitents, expounding the Scriptures in private houses, and often preaching in the open air, sometimes to twenty thousand persons. If it be asked how he was enabled to accomplish so much, he himself distinctly answers that "he received assistance from above. He lived in the spirit of prayer; he laid hold upon the strength Divine by a mighty faith, and he realized the fulfillment of the promise, I am with you always."

For some years from this time, Charles Wesley is represented as a prince of preachers, surpassed by no other man since the apostolic times in power and efficiency, and the people everywhere fell under his word like grass under the scythe of the mower.

Here we have a picture of one of these great assemblies, drawn by the minister:

"Thousands," writes Charles, "stood in the churchyard. It was the most beautiful sight I ever beheld. The people filled the gradually rising area, which was shut upon three sides by a vast perpendicular hill. On the top and bottom of this hill was a circular row of trees.

In this amphitheater they stood, deeply attentive, while I called upon them, in Christ's words, 'Come unto me all that are weary.' The tears of many testified that they were ready to enter into that rest. God enabled me to lift up my voice like a trumpet, so that all distinctly heard me. I concluded with singing an invitation to sinners. It was with difficulty we made our way through this most loving people, and returned, amid their prayers and blessings, to Ebley."

Here we have a picture of a similar scene, drawn by another than the minister, by a Calvinist Dissenter:

"Hearing that Mr. Charles Wesley would preach in the afternoon just out of the city, I got a guide, and went to hear him. I found him standing upon a table, in an erect posture, with his hands and eyes lifted up to heaven in prayer, surrounded with, I guess, more than a thousand people; some few of them persons of fashion, both men and women, but most of them of the lower rank of mankind. I know not how long he had been engaged in the duty before I came, but he continued therein, after my coming, scarcely a quarter of an hour, during which time he prayed with uncommon fervency, fluency, and variety of proper expression. He then preached about an hour, from 2 Cor. v, 17–21, in such a manner as I have seldom, if ever, heard any minister preach; that is, though I have heard many a finer sermon, according to the common taste, yet I have scarcely ever heard any minister discover such evident signs of a most vehement desire, or labor so earnestly to convince his hearers that they were all by nature in a state of enmity against God, consequently in a damnable state, and needed reconciliation to God; that God is willing to be reconciled to all, even the worst of sinners, and for that end hath laid all our sin on Christ, and Christ hath borne the punishment due to our sins in our nature and stead; that, on the other hand, the righteousness and merits of Christ are imparted to as many as believe on him; that it is faith alone, exclusive entirely of any works of ours, which applies to us the righteousness of Christ, and justifies us in the sight of God; that none are excluded but those who refuse to come to him as lost, undone, yea, as damned sinners, and trust in him alone, that is, in his meritorious righteousness and atoning sacrifice, for pardon and salvation. These points he supported all along, as he went on, with many texts of Scripture, which he explained and illustrated; and then freely invited all, even the chief of sinners, and used a great variety of the most moving arguments and expostulations, in order to persuade, allure, instigate, and, if possible, compel all to come to Christ, and believe in him for pardon and salvation.

"Nor did he fail to inform them thoroughly, how ineffectual their faith would be to justify them in the sight of God, unless it wrought by love, purified their hearts, and reformed their lives; for though he cautioned them, with the utmost care, not to attribute any merit to their own performances, nor in the least degree rest upon any works of their own; yet, at the same time, he apprized them that their faith is but a dead faith if it be not operative and productive of good works, even all the good in their power."

The same hand describes, as follows, a subsequent evening meeting of one of the societies, when Charles Wesley prayed and expounded:

"Never did I hear such praying, or such singing—never did I see and hear such evident marks of fervency of spirit in the service of God—as in that society. At the close of every single petition, a serious amen, like a rushing sound of waters, ran through the whole society; and their singing was not only the most harmonious and delightful I ever heard, but, as Mr. Whitefield writes in his Journals, they 'sung lustily, and with a good courage.' I never so well understood the meaning of that expression before. Indeed, they seemed to sing with melody in their hearts. It is impossible for any man to try another's heart; neither would I dare to invade the Divine prerogative; but this I will venture to say: such evident marks of a lively, genuine devotion, in any part of religious worship, I never was witness to in any place, or on any occasion. If there be such a thing as heavenly music upon earth, I heard it there. If there be such an employment, such an attainment, as that of a heaven upon earth, numbers in that society seem to possess it. As for my own part, I do not remember my heart to have been so elevated in prayer and praise, either in collegiate, parochial, or private worship, as it was there and then."

## OPPOSITION.

THE extraordinary career in which Charles Wesley and his brother John were now fully launched failed not to excite stern opposition, and that, too, from various sources. Their field-preaching, and their more private assemblies for worship, and for the revival of religion, came under the ban of the Church authorities, as being irregular and unlawful. At the same time, the great central doctrine of *salvation by faith* seemed equally distasteful to theologues and carnal professors. Also their pungent and powerful addresses in preaching, and the earnestness and fervor with which they pressed the necessity of regeneration in order to salvation, kindled fierce opposition among the high and the low. Still further, the multiplication of converts, and the spirit of religious inquiry that was awakened in various places, provoked opposition from not a few.

One or two brief illustrations may, perhaps, entertain the reader.

Charles is summoned into the presence of the Archbishop of Canterbury. He is proceeding to make a statement.*

*Archbishop.* I do not dispute. What call have you?

*Charles.* A dispensation of the Gospel is committed to me.

*A.* That is, to St. Paul; but I do not dispute, *and will not proceed to excommunicate yet.*

* See Frontispiece.

*C.* Your grace has taught me, in your book on Church government, that a man unjustly excommunicated is not thereby cast off from communion with Christ.

*A.* Of that I am the judge.

*C.* Is not Mr. Whitefield's success a spiritual sign, and sufficient proof of his call

The archbishop's reply to this question is not given, but he dismisses Charles from his presence with every mark of displeasure.

This dark and threatening interview was on Thursday. Charles returned from the palace in peace, and on the very next Sabbath preached in the open air at Moorfields to ten thousand sinners. This was in the morning. In the afternoon, on Kennington Common, he preached again to an immense multitude.

We are here reminded of the apostle, as in view of threatening perils he exclaimed: "None of these things move me, neither count I my life dear unto myself so that I may finish my course with joy, and the ministry I have received of the Lord Jesus to testify the Gospel of the grace of God."

The archbishop talked of excommunication; "but," says Mr. Jackson, "he reconsidered the subject, and wisely forbore to execute his threat. Perhaps he recollected that the Son of God preached upon a mountain, and on a plain, and addressed multitudes on the sea-shore as he sat in a fishing-boat; and that the apostle of the Gentiles preached Jesus and the resurrection to the inquisitive Athenians as he stood upon Mars' hill. It would indeed have been an unseemly thing for a man invested with ecclesiastical authority, and professing to derive that authority from the Lord Jesus, in a direct line from the apostles, to impose silence upon Christian ministers, and even expel them from the congregation of the faithful, for doing that which the Lord himself, and the holy apostles under his direct sanction, had recommended by their daily practice. The Protestant Church of England was preserved from the deep dishonor of an act so thoroughly antichristian."

The following presents a specimen of opposition of a somewhat different character:

Charles goes to Bengeworth and calls for his friend, Mr. Seward. He being sick, sends his brother Henry in his stead, who, coming into Charles's presence, charges him with the downfall of his brother, picking his pockets, ruining his family, and proceeds to call him a scoundrel and rascal, and threatens to whip him. Much other disturbance and abuse follow from this impudent young man, when, on a subsequent visit to the place, Charles and Henry meet again.

*Henry.* Please step into the Crown.

*Charles.* I do not frequent taverns.

*H.* What business have you with my brother?

*C.* Can you imagine, if I have any business with him as a Christian, I shall communicate it to you?

*H.* Why not to me?

*C.* Because you are a natural man.

*H.* Why are not you a natural man, as well as I?

*C.* You are a *mere* natural man, in your sins, and in your blood.

*H.* What do you mean by that? I say, have you any particular business?

*C.* I have business at present somewhat different from talking with you.

Thus ended the interview, and the next day the two met again, when Henry apologized for his past behavior, and excused himself by saying that anger was rooted in his nature.

*Henry.* But indeed, sir, you are the downfall of my brother Benjamin. He has certainly been out of his senses.

*Charles.* Yes, and so have I been before now in a fever.

*H.* O, but we all really think him mad, through means of you.

*C.* Very likely you may; and if it should ever please God to make you a Christian, you will be thought mad too.

*H.* God make me a Christian! I am a better Christian than you are.

*C.* You was once in the way of being one, but you have stifled your convictions.

*H.* I say I am a better Christian than you are. I have good ministers and the Scriptures to teach me.

*C.* Yes; and those Scriptures say a man that loves money is no more a Christian than an adulterer.

*H.* What, sir, must not a man love money? How shall he go to market without it? Not that I value it, not I. But what do you mean by making divisions in our family? You come now to get money.

*C.* Indeed, sir, you know not what I come for; you judge me by your own standard; money is your God, and you think I come to rob you of it.

*H.* You are a rascal, a villain, and a pick-pocket.

But Charles was compelled to encounter opposition of a much more painful character. We have seen, in the pages preceding, how great a blessing his ministry had proved to the Delamotte family.

Will it be believed that all of these, under the influence of the German quietism, had turned aside from the ordinances and the faith of the Gospel? Charles visited them at Blendon, with some faint hope of reclaiming them to their first faith and love. As he endeavored to reason with the deluded mother and daughters, they repeatedly bade him be silent. At length Charles said: "Do you therefore, at this time, in the presence of Jesus Christ, acquit, release, and discharge me from any further care, concern, or regard for your souls? Do you desire I would never more speak unto you in his name?' Betty frankly answered, 'Yes.' Mrs. Delamotte assented by her silence. 'Then here,' said I, 'I take my leave of you, till we meet at the judgment-seat!' With these words I rendered up my charge to God.

"'Then,' said I, after leaving them, 'I have labored in vain; I have spent my strength for naught: yet surely my judgment is with the Lord, and my work with my God. Surely this is enough to wean and make me cease from man. With Blendon I give up all expectation of gratitude upon earth. Vanity of vanities, all is vanity; even friendship itself!'"

Such are but a specimen. It was emphatically true of the Wesleys, that a great and effectual door was opened unto them, but there were many adversaries.

---

## INCIDENTS.

Yet amid all opposition Charles is not discouraged; his earnest and buoyant spirit towers above discouragements, and glides over tumults and obstacles as easily as the floating sea-bird rises over the waves of the surging ocean.

Sprightly and pleasant are the notices dropping from his pen of his preachings and varied exercises and movements.

One summer day he preached five times in as many different places, and writes that "preaching five times a day, when God calls me to it, no more wears the flesh than preaching once." One of these sermons was at Bath. "Satan took it ill," he says, "to be attacked in his own quarters—that Sodom of our land. While I was explaining the trembling jailer's question, he raged horribly in his children. They went out and came back again, and mocked, and at last roared, as if each man's name was Legion. My power increased with the opposition."

He preached in Porthkerry, in Wales. "God was among us," said he, "and a mighty tempest was stirred up round about him. Never hath he given me more convincing words. The poor simple souls fell down at the feet of Jesus."

He encounters a clergyman, Mr. Carne, who is offended at the multitude that flock to Charles's preaching. He stands up during all the sermon of two hours, and is compelled to see the great company of mourners, and the abundance of tears under the sermon. After service he says to Charles: "Sir, you have got very good lungs, but you will make the people melancholy. I saw them crying throughout the church." Then Carne turned to the gentleman that entertained Charles, saying: "You will make yourself ridiculous all over the country by encouraging such a fellow."

He goes to a revel in a certain town, and endeavors to dissuade them from what they deem their *innocent* diversions. An old dame of threescore falls down under the stroke of the hammer, who could never before be convinced of the harm of dancing.

He preaches to some prisoners under sentence of death. The most hardened one, of which he had the least hope, appears truly justified, and declares that he has no fears of death, and no ill-will toward his persecutors. "But have you not had any fear of death?" "Yes," he replied, "till I heard you preach; then it went away, and I have felt no trouble ever since.'

He visits a magistrate at Kingswood, who was the most forward of all the adversaries there, and had threatened seizure of their school for the colliers.

*Charles.* I came to wait upon you in respect to your office, having heard that you were offended at the good we were doing to the poor colliers. I should be sorry to give you any just cause of complaint.

*Justice.* Your school here would make a good work-house.

*C.* It is a work-house already.

*J.* Aye, but what work is done there?

*C.* We work the works of God, which man cannot hinder.

*J.* But you occasion the increase of our poor.

*C.* Sir, you are misinformed; the reverse of that is true. None of our society is chargeable to you; even those who were so before they heard us, who spent all their wages at the ale-house, now never go there at all, but keep their money to maintain their families, and have to give to those who want. Notorious swearers have now only the praises of God in their mouths. The good done among them is indisputable: our worst enemies can't deny it. None who hear us continue either to swear or drink.

*J.* If I thought so I would come and hear you myself.

*C.* Come! the grace of God is as sufficient for you as for our colliers.

*J.* I shall not at all concern myself, for if what you do you do for gain, you have your reward; if for the sake of God, he will recompense you. I am of Gamaliel's mind: "If this work be of men it will come to naught."

*C.* "But if it be of God ye cannot overthrow it; lest, haply, ye be found to fight against God." Therefore follow Gamaliel's advice: "Take heed to yourselves; refrain from these men, and let them alone."

"He seemed determined so to do," adds Charles; "and thus, through the blessing of God, we parted friends."

At St. Ives, Charles hears the rector preach. The application of his sermon is downright railing at the "new sect," "the enemies of the Church, seducers, troublers, scribes and pharisees, hypocrites." Charles keeps a quiet heart and steady countenance.

At Wednock he hears a curate preach, and his text is "Beware of false prophets" "I stood over against him," writes Charles, "within two yards of the pulpit, and heard such a hotch-potch of railing, foolish lies, as Satan himself might have been ashamed of. I had asked that my countenance might not alter, and was kept in perfect peace. The poor people behaved very decently, and all followed me to hear the true word of God. I stayed, and mildly told the preacher he had been misinformed. 'No,' he answered; 'it was all truth.' 'Sir,' said I, 'if you believe what you preach you believe a lie.' 'You are a liar,' he replied. I put him in mind of the great day, testified my good-will, and left him."

## PERSECUTIONS.

Five years had now passed since the Wesleys had obtained the precious faith of the Gospel, and had entered upon their peculiar ministry, proclaiming earnestly and in multitudes of places the great salvation by Christ. We have seen that opposition had already arrayed itself against them, and it is a most significant and melancholy fact that this opposition commenced in the heart of the Church of which they were accredited ministers. They were soon excluded from most of the pulpits of the Established Church, while in many places the clergy were not satisfied with withdrawing from them all ministerial courtesy, but were concerned, in connection with magistrates, in stirring up the rabble to the most violent and disgraceful opposition.

Charles Wesley, for example, is at Walsal. He walks through the town amid the noisy greetings of enemies. As he preaches, standing on the steps of the market-house, "the floods lifted up their voices and raged horribly. The streets were full of fierce Ephesian beasts, who roared, and shouted, and threw stones incessantly. Many struck without hurting me. I besought them in calm love to be reconciled to God in Christ. While I was departing a stream of ruffians was suffered to bear me from the steps. I rose, and having given the blessing, was beaten down again."

In Sheffield the clergy had succeeded in inflaming the public mind, so that during his stay a mob assembled and pulled down the Methodist chapel, which had been erected by the liberality of a poor people.

He goes to the society house to preach, and "hell from beneath is moved to oppose him. No sooner does he enter the desk than the floods lift up their voice. An officer contradicted and blasphemed. The preacher takes no notice of him, but sings on. Meanwhile the stones fly on, hitting the desk and people. The preacher gives notice that he will preach in the

CHARLES WESLEY IN A MOB.

open air; and as he goes out the whole army of aliens follow him, and he preaches the Gospel with much contention, the stones often hitting him in the face while he is speaking. The sermon being finished, Charles prays for sinners as servants of their master, the devil. Whereupon the officer rushes upon him with great fury, threatening revenge, draws his sword and points it at the breast of the minister. "My breast was immediately steeled. I threw it open, and fixing mine eye on his, smiled in his face, and calmly said, 'I fear God, and honor the king.' His countenance fell in a moment; he fetched a deep sigh, put up his sword, and quickly left the place."

They followed Charles to his lodgings, and greater outrages succeeded through the night. "They pressed hard," said Charles, "to break open the door. I would have gone out to them, but the brethren would not suffer me. They labored all night for their master, and by morning had pulled down one end of the house. I could compare them to nothing but the men of

Sodom; or those coming out of the tombs, 'exceeding fierce.' Their outcries often waked me in the night: yet I believe I got more sleep than any of my neighbors."

The next day this undaunted soldier of Christ proposes to preach in the heart of the town, and went forth nothing doubting. As he goes, he hears the enemy shouting from afar. He stands up in the midst of the multitude and proclaims, "If God be for us, who can be against us." He adds: "God made bare his arm in the sight of the heathen, and so restrained the fierceness of men, that not one lifted up hand or voice against us."

After preaching he retires to his lodgings through the open street, with the multitude at his heels. As he passes he sees the preaching-house, with "not one stone upon another," and as he looks he reminds himself that "the foundation of God standeth sure," and thinks of the house not made with hands, eternal in the heavens.

All is quiet till he enters his lodgings. Then

the mob renew their violence, threatening to level the house to the ground; the windows are smashed in an instant, and the poor owner, in his fright, seems "ready to give up his shield." Yet the rebels were overawed; one of the sturdiest of them was captured, and carried into the house, and in a few minutes the hated and despised minister was wrapped in sweet sleep, in the very room which the mob had just dismantled. "I feared no cold," he said, "but dropped asleep with that word, 'Scatter thou the people that delight in war.'"

Thence Charles goes to Thorpe, having been notified that the people of that place were exceeding mad against him. Approaching the town, an ambush of rowdies suddenly arose from their concealment, and assault him with stones, eggs, and mud. With much difficulty he and his traveling companion force their way through the mob. Returning to them, he asks the reason a clergyman may not pass without such treatment. At first they scatter; then their captain, rallying them, answers with horrible imprecations, and stones that would have killed both man and beast, had they not been turned aside by an unseen hand.

Charles's horse takes fright and runs away with him, the rabble following with hideous shoutings. Yet he finds a place of refuge, "meets many sincere souls assembled to hear the word of God. Never have I known a greater power of love. All were drowned in tears, yet very happy. . . . We rejoiced in the God of our salvation, who hath compassed us about with songs of deliverance." About six weeks afterward Charles is at St. Ives, walking toward the market-house for the purpose of preaching to the multitudes. When we came to the place of battle the enemy was ready, set in array against us. I began the hundredth psalm, and they beating their drums and shouting. I stood still and silent for some time, finding they would not receive my testimony. I then offered to speak to some of the most violent; but they stopped their ears and ran upon me, crying, I should not preach there, and catching at me to pull me down. They had no power to touch me. My soul was calm and fearless. I shook off the dust of my feet, and walked leisurely through the thickest of them, who followed like ramping and roaring lions. But their mouth was shut. We met the mayor, who saluted us, and threatened the rioters. I rejoiced at my lodgings in one almighty Jesus."

One specimen more must suffice, and it shall be given in Charles's own words:

"I had just named my text at St. Ives, 'Comfort ye, comfort ye my people, saith your God!' when an army of rebels broke in upon us, like those at Sheffield or Wednesbury. They began in a most outrageous manner, threatening to murder the people if they did not go out that moment. They broke the sconces, dashed the windows in pieces, bore away the shutters, benches, poor-box, and all but the stone walls.

"I stood silently looking on, but my eyes were unto the Lord. They swore bitterly I should not preach there again; which I immediately disproved by telling them Christ died for them all. Several times they lifted up their hands and clubs to strike me; but a stronger arm restrained them. They beat and dragged the women about, particularly one of a great age, and trampled on them without mercy.

"The longer they stayed, and the more they raged, the more power I found from above. I bade the people stand still and see the salvation of God, resolving to continue with them and see the end.

"In about an hour the word came, 'Hitherto shalt thou come, and no further.' The ruffians fell to quarreling among themselves, broke the town clerk's (their captain's) head, and drove one another out of the room.

"Having kept the field, we gave thanks for the victory, and in prayer the Spirit of glory rested upon us."

Thus it was that for a series of years the Wesleys, in the strong evangelical career which they had undertaken, were doomed to encounter opposition and persecution worthy of the gloom and fanaticism of the dark ages. Spiritual religion in the Establishment, and among Dissenters, was at a low ebb. The land seems to have been greatly given up to drunkenness, rioting, and violence. Police regulations and restrictions were loosely and partially administered; and in most cases the ministers of justice were enemies of the evangelical movement, and often took sides with the mob, and refused to defend the oppressed ministers and people.

"I preached," writes Charles, "near Penzance, to the little flock, encompassed by ravening wolves. Their minister rages above measure against this new sect, who are spread throughout his four livings. His reverend brethren follow his example. The grossest lies which are brought them they swallow without examination, and retail the following Sunday. One of the society, James Duke, went lately to the worshipful the Rev. Dr. Borlase for justice against a rioter who had broken open his house and stolen his goods. The doctor's answer was: 'Thou conceited fellow! art thou turned religions? They may burn thy house if they will. Thou shalt have no justice.' With these words he drove him from the judgment-seat."

Under date of next day, he writes again:

"One of our sisters complained to the mayor of some who had thrown into her house stones of many pounds weight, which fell on the pillow within a few inches of her sucking child. The magistrate cursed her, and said, 'You shall have no justice here. You see there is none for you at London, or you would have got it before now.' With this saying he drove her out of his house."

But enough of these sickening details. Yet it is well that the young should have some view, though it be but a glimpse, of the terrible and constant opposition and the multiplied sufferings under which the Wesleyan Reformation arose, and against which it triumphed gloriously.

## THE GWYNNES.

Charles Wesley was now forty years of age, and was as yet unmarried. Ten years he had been occupied, in connection with his brother John, in a most arduous and prosperous ministry; yet a ministry of such a peculiar character as to appear to render it inexpedient to encumber themselves with families.

"I have always had a fear," said Charles, "but no *thought* of marrying for many years past, even from my first preaching the Gospel."

He immediately adds, however: "But within this twelvemonth that thought has forced itself in: 'How know I whether it be best for me to marry or no?' Certainly better now than later; and if not now, what security that I shall not then? It should be now or not at all."

Far away in Wales, amid a beautiful and charming retreat, lived *Marmaduke Gwynne, Esq.*, a gentleman of family and fortune, who had been greatly benefited under the ministry of the celebrated Howell Harris. He was "a man of fine spirit, deeply pious, kind to his tenantry, beneficent to the poor, and exemplary in all the relations of life."

His establishment was large and princely. His wife was one of six heiresses, each of whom had a fortune of $150,000, and each was married into a family of rank. She was a lady of large understanding and generous impulses, yet of a proud heart. Greatly averse, at first, to Mr. Harris and the religious influence he exerted upon her husband, she subsequently laid aside her prejudices, was induced to read and hear for herself, and became a friend and partaker of spiritual Christianity.

Nine sons and daughters, twenty servants, a chaplain, and nurse constituted the establishment of the Gwynnes. The Church service, both for the morning and evening, was daily read. More or less guests, of great respectability, were almost always present; and altogether it was one of those magnificent and lovely homes for which England is so much distinguished.

*Sarah Gwynne* was one of the daughters of this bright home. She was beautiful in person, and of genial temper and peaceful manners; moreover she possessed deep and genuine piety, and had renounced the world, with its gayeties and pleasures, for the sake of Christ and salvation.

The ministry of Harris had been of special benefit to Sarah, as also that of the Wesleys, who, in their extensive travels, had been received at her father's mansion as the angels of God.

It was delightful to this young lady to accompany, with her father, these evangelists in their preaching excursions in the adjoining country; and both father and daughter had made a long visit to the Wesleys, at the Foundry, in London, and had witnessed the vast congregation, and been delighted with the spirituality and earnestness of the worship there, and with the evident reality and greatness of the work of God of which the two devoted brothers had been the chief instrumentality.

It is needless to add that this was the beautiful and excellent young lady who had won the heart of Charles Wesley.

Yet nothing had been disclosed to her, or any of the family, on the subject. Every successive visit had served to strengthen his attachment, and his persuasion that, in the event of his marrying, Sarah would be the most suitable object of his choice.

"When Charles and his brother returned from Georgia, they entered into an agreement that neither of them would marry, or take any direct step toward marriage, without the knowledge and consent of the other. On his arrival in London, in November, 1748, he fulfilled his part of the covenant by informing his brother that it was his intention to offer himself as the future husband of Miss Gwynne. He was agreeably surprised to find that his brother not only offered no objection, but had actually anticipated his wishes in this affair. John had entertained the thought of recommending to Charles three young ladies of their acquaintance, any one of whom he deemed suitable for

Charles's wife; and Miss Gwynne was one of the number, so that he decidedly approved the choice which Charles had made. They consulted together concerning every particular, and were of one heart and mind in all things."

Thus encouraged, Charles immediately proceeded to Wales, to solicit the heart and hand of Miss Gwynne. "It was an understanding between him and his brother that a refusal from the young lady, or even one of her parents, should be regarded as an absolute prohibition, and the suit should be forever abandoned.

"Happily for him, his former attentions to Miss Gwynne, and the sterling excellences which she had long seen in him, had already won her affections. The matter was then disclosed to the mother by Miss Becky Gwynne, another of the daughters, who was also in favor of the match.

"Mrs. Gwynne answered, 'I would rather give my child to Mr. Wesley than to any man in England.' She afterward spoke to him with great friendliness, and said that she had 'no manner of objection but the want of fortune.'

"At the same time Mr. Gwynne gave his free and unhesitating consent, and left all the arrangements to his wife, who was well qualified for the task by her natural shrewdness and business habits."

Delighted with his success, the happy lover took a friendly leave of the Gwynnes, and returned to London to receive the congratulations of his brother for his prosperous journey.

## MARRIAGE.

Having, by the kind assistance of his brother John, secured the required annuity of one hundred pounds, Charles Wesley set out with a light and glad heart for Wales. His brother and another friend accompanied him.

"When the party arrived at Garth, they found Mr. Howell Gwynne, the eldest brother of Sarah, visiting the family, and vehemently opposed to the union of his sister with a Methodist clergyman. The mother expostulated with him, and Miss Becky told him point blank that he ought to consider the offer of his sister's suitor an honor done to himself as one of the family."

It is added, however, that this brother was soon divested of his hostility, and became as affable and friendly as the rest of the family.

On this visit the necessary preliminaries were definitely settled, and it was agreed that the marriage should be solemnized within two months.

"During this interval Mr. Charles Wesley applied himself to his ministerial labor with unabated diligence and zeal; and at the same time he carried on a correspondence with Miss Gwynne, remarkable for its piety. A considerable part of his letters to her were written in verse—a vehicle in which his thoughts flowed in the most natural manner, especially when his feelings were excited.

"These compositions are exceedingly animated, and breathe the most pure and fervent devotion. They call upon the object of his affection, to whom he now stood in so tender a relation, to unite with him in an unreserved dedication of herself to their common Saviour; and express many fears lest the love of the creature should at all interfere with that supreme love to God which is the very end of the commandment, and therefore the soul of religion. Never was wedded love more strong and decided than that which he cherished, and never was it more thoroughly sanctified by a perfect and constant reference to God, who has instituted marriage for purposes connected with his own glory."

The eighth day of April, 1749, was the marriage day of Charles Wesley. He, in company with his brother, had arrived at the mansion of the Gwynnes several days before, and all matters had been arranged satisfactorily. John, it appears, had entertained some scruples touching the possible effect of his brother's marriage upon his usefulness as an itinerant preacher, and was not without fear that he might thus be deprived of Charles's assistance in the great revival of religion that was now spreading itself over the land.

His doubts and scruples were, however, removed, and in his Journal, under the above date, we notice the characteristic entry following:

"I married my brother and Sarah Gwynne. It was a solemn day, such as became the dignity of a Christian marriage."

Charles' own entry is equally characteristic:

"Saturday, April 8th, 1749.

"'Sweet day, so cool, so calm, so bright,—
The bridal of the earth and sky.'

"Not a cloud was to be seen from morning till night. I rose at four, spent three hours and a half in prayer, or singing, with my brother, with Sally, and with Beck. At eight I led my Sally to church. Her father, sisters, Lady Rudd, Grace Bowen, Betty Williams, and, I think, Billy Tucker and Mr. James, were all the persons present. Mr. Gwynne gave her to me under God. My brother joined our hands. It was a most solemn season of love! I never had more of the Divine presence at the sacrament.

My brother gave out a hymn. He then prayed over us in strong faith. We walked back to the house and joined again in prayer. Prayer and thanksgiving was our whole employment. We were cheerful without mirth—serious without sadness. A stranger that intermeddleth not with our joy, said it looked more like a funeral than a wedding. My brother seemed the happiest person among us."

The account adds that the happy bridegroom remained about two weeks with the Gwynnes after his marriage, preaching every morning and evening, either in the mansion of his father-in-law or in the neighboring towns and villages. He then resumed his itinerant ministry. Under date of April 29, three weeks after his marriage, he writes of severe illness having been caused by an extreme eagerness to prosecute his ministry. "I was," he says, "too eager for the work, and therefore believe God checked me by that short sickness."

## THE EARTHQUAKE.

Charles Wesley was eminently fortunate and happy in his marriage, and bright and blissful days now shone over him. He seems to have craved nothing save the glory of God in the salvation of men.

Soon after his marriage he rented a small house in Bristol and commenced housekeeping. It seems to have been such an abode as suited "a stranger and a pilgrim upon earth." "I saw my house," he writes, "and consecrated it by prayer and thanksgiving. . . . At six our first guests passed a useful hour with us. I preached on the first words I met, Rom. xii, 1. The power and blessing of God were with us. At half past nine I slept comfortably in my own house, yet not my own."

Meanwhile his Journal of these days speaks of tears, amid his retired walks, in view of the Divine goodness. He tells of being greatly blessed in his private devotions. "In a word," he says, "whatsoever I do prospers."

Yet while he was signally blessed in his ministry, he seems to have been, at times, subject to strong mental depression. "To this, indeed, he was constitutionally prone, and from this period to the end of his life he was more or less affected by it. When he was daily employed in preaching and in traveling from place to place, he was carried above all feelings of despondency, and lived in a state of high spiritual enjoyment. But when he sat down in domestic quiet, those feelings often returned in unabated power.

On the eighth of February, 1750, the Wesleys both speak of an earthquake in London. Just one month afterward another shock was felt, far more violent than the first. Charles was just naming his text for preaching at the Foundry, when the building shook so violently that every one supposed it would fall upon their heads. A great tumult ensued, when the preacher cried out: "Therefore will not we fear though the earth be removed, and the hills be carried into the midst of the sea; for the

Lord of Hosts is with us, the God of Jacob is our refuge." He adds: "The Lord filled my heart with faith, and my mouth with words, shaking their souls as well as their bodies."

This earthquake appears to have been felt specially in London and Westminster. It was a strong and jarring motion, attended with a rumbling noise, like that of distant thunder. Many houses were much shaken, and some chimneys thrown down, but without any further hurt. The alarm which it occasioned, as might be supposed, was deep and general, many apprehending a return of the calamity in a more destructive form."

Touching the same event Charles Wesley writes thus to his wife:

"My dearest, dearest Friend—Grace and peace be multiplied upon you and yours, who are mine also.

"One letter a week does not half satisfy me under your absence. I count the days since we parted, and those still between us and our next meeting. Yet I dare not promise myself the certain blessing, so many are the evils and accidents of life. Accidents I should not call them; for God ordereth all things in heaven and earth.

"Who knows His will concerning this wicked city? or how near we may be to the fate of Lima or Portugal?

"Blessed be God, many consider this day of danger and adversity. The Bishop of London has published a seasonable, solemn warning. Our churches are crowded as at the beginning."

It was at this time that Charles preached the discourse entitled, "Cause and Cure of Earthquakes," published in the first volume of the American edition of Wesley's Sermons.

He also composed several hymns under the title of "Hymns occasioned by the Earthquake, March 8th, 1750." These breathe a spirit similar to that of the sermon, describing in strong and glowing terms the power and sovereignty of God, his merciful and righteous government over men, national and personal sins, the divine forbearance and long-suffering, the uncertainty of life, and of all earthly possessions, and the durable nature of the joys which are connected with Christian godliness, both in time and eternity."

In opposition to a letter that had been published concerning the earthquake, referring the event to second causes merely, and ignoring any agency of God in the matter, Charles Wesley thus sings:

"From whence these dire portents around,
 That strike us with unwonted fear?
Why do these earthquakes rock the ground,
 And threaten our destruction near?
Ye prophets smooth the cause explain,
And lull us to repose again.

"Or water swelling for a vent,
 Or air impatient to get free,
Or fire within earth's entrails pent,"
 Yet all are order'd, Lord, by thee;
The elements obey thy nod,
And nature vindicates her God.

"The pillars of the earth are thine,
 And thou hast set the world thereon;
They at thy threat'ning look incline,
 The center trembles at thy frown;
The everlasting mountains bow,
And God is in the earthquake *now*.

"Now, Lord, to shake a guilty land
  Thou dost in indignation rise;
We see, we see thy lifted hand,
  Made bare a nation to chastise,
When neither plagues nor mercies move
To fear thy wrath, or court thy love.

"Therefore the earth beneath us reels,
  And staggers like our drunken men;
The earth the mournful cause reveals,
  And groans our burden to sustain;
Ordain'd our evils to deplore,
And fall with us to rise no more."

## CORRESPONDENCE.

Charles Wesley's itinerant labors became, after his marriage, more circumscribed than formerly. At length his ministry was confined mostly to the important points of London and Bristol.

It was at the latter city that he had taken up his residence, and this involved his absence from his family so much of the time as he was occupied in London.

During his separation from his wife, his letters to her were very frequent, and were strongly marked by that deep and tender affection which ever characterized him as a husband. They also indicate his zeal and faithfulness as an embassador of the Lord Jesus.

The following brief extracts are culled from the pages of this correspondence:

"Your illness would quite overwhelm me were I not assured that it should work together for your good, and enhance your happiness through eternity. How does this assurance change the nature of things!

'Sorrow is joy, and pain is ease,
If thou, my God, art here.'

The slightest suffering received from Him is an inestimable blessing, another jewel added to your crown. Go, then, my faithful partner, doing and suffering His blessed will, till out of great tribulation we both enter his kingdom, and his joy, and his glory everlasting."

"May the choicest blessings of God go along with these lines, and meet you well at Ludlow! On Friday I trust he will grant me my heart's desire, even the sight of one I love next to himself."

"My strength is as my day. George Whitefield has taken off great part of my labor. I let him preach yesterday at the chapel, reserving myself for the watch-night. In consideration whereof we had service this morning an hour later. These things I mention in proof of my great carefulness, and in hope you will follow a good example."

"My dearest partner, abide under the shadow of the Almighty. Let us trust him for each other. He never faileth them that seek him; and whoso putteth his trust in the Lord, mercy embraceth him on every side."

"Mr. Fletcher read prayers again in the afternoon. I testified, 'If the Son shall make you free, ye shall be free indeed.' Our chapel was crowded as on Fast-day. Lady Huntingdon, Lady Gertrude, Mrs. Cartaret, and a multitude of strangers attended. I continued my discourse for a whole hour, the Lord being my strength, and giving me utterance."

"I passed two useful hours at Miss Bosanquet's, [afterward Mrs. Fletcher.] Eight orphans she has taken to train up for God."

"Can I *threaten* my bosom friend with any evil? No; but I sometimes mind her of that blessed day when we shall put off these tabernacles. But I do not think we shall be long divided. Yet if it gives you pain, I shall endeavor to forbear."

"Yours of August 13th has just now brought me the mournful news of your increasing illness. Yet would I say, 'It is the Lord; let him do what seemeth him good!' Still my hope of you is steadfast, that hereby you shall be partaker of his holiness, who, in kindest love, chastens you for your good; and you may be bold to say, 'When he hath tried me I shall come forth as gold.'"

"I am come from preaching to a most attentive multitude. This place seems quite subdued to our Lord. Their hearts are all bowed before him. He gives me uncommon strength. A very great door is opened. The poor people have got in their harvest, and are now at leisure to be gathered in themselves. The heavens smile upon us, and the weather seems made on purpose for preaching."

"My bodily strength increases the more I use it for the Lord. Every day brings its blessings, both to me and to those that hear me. It is pleasant traveling with such an errand. Nothing but the company of my true yokefellow could make it pleasanter. The *next* time you hinder me in my work will be the *first* time. . . . Let us join with greater earnestness than ever to seek the kingdom of God together."

"Who is your chaplain? When none is near, you should read prayers yourself, as my mother and many besides have done. Be much in private prayer. What the Lord will do with me I know not; but am fully persuaded I shall not long survive my brother. Farewell."

## SORROWS.

The last sentence of the preceding chapter alludes to a desperate illness of Mr. John Wesley, with which he was seized toward the close of 1753. He and all his friends supposed it to be a settled consumption, and his case was generally thought to be hopeless. "His symptoms were those of confirmed consumption, being a cough, pain in the breast, fever, with loss of strength."

It may well be supposed that Charles Wesley was very deeply affected at the heavy tidings concerning his brother. He thus addresses his absent wife upon the subject:

"But first you expect news of my brother. He is at Lewisham, considerably better, yet still in imminent danger, being far gone and very suddenly in a consumption. I cannot acquit my friends of unpardonable negligence, since not one of them sent me word of his condition, but left me to hear it by chance. I hasten to him to-morrow morning.

"I found him," he writes again, "with my sister, and Mrs. Blackwell, and Dewal. I fell on his neck and wept. All present were alike affected. Last Wednesday he changed for the better, while the people were praying for him at the Foundry. He has rested well ever since; his cough is abated, and his strength increased. Yet it is most probable he will not recover, being far gone in a galloping consumption, just as my elder brother was at his age. I followed him to his chamber with my sister, and prayed with strong desire and a good hope of his recovery. All last Tuesday they expected his death every hour; he expected the same, and wrote his own epitaph:

"'Here lieth the body of John Wesley, a brand plucked out of the fire. He died of a consumption, in the fifty-first year of his age, leaving, after his debts were paid, not ten pounds behind him; praying, *God be merciful to me an unprofitable servant!*' He desired this inscription, if any, should be put upon his tombstone."

A day or two afterward, Charles again writes to his wife as follows:

"I hope you have recovered your fright. My brother may live if he hastens to Bristol. Prayer is made daily by the Church to God for him."

And these prayers were answered; and John Wesley came up from his consumption, and for nearly forty years longer preached most earnestly, diligently, and successfully the Gospel of Christ.

A few days after his brother John began to recover, Charles received the mournful intelligence that his beloved wife was seized with the small-pox. He immediately left London for home, and arrived on the afternoon of the following day.

"I found my dearest friend," he writes, "on a restless bed of pain, loaded with the worst kind of the worst disease. . . . . She had expressed a longing desire to see me just before I came, and rejoiced for the consolation. I saw her alive, but O how changed! 'The whole head is sick, and the whole heart faint! From the sole of the foot even unto the head, there is no soundness in her; but wounds and putrifying sores.'

"Yet under her sorest burden she blessed God that she had not been inoculated, receiving the disease as immediately sent from God. I found the door of prayer wide open, and entirely acquiesced in the divine will; I would not have it otherwise. God choose for me and mine in time and eternity."

Twenty-two days did Mrs. Wesley hang between life and death under this most terrible disease.

"A part of this anxious time her husband was compelled to spend in London, supplying the chapels there, his afflicted brother being still laid aside from his ministry. He preached comfort to others while his own heart was sad, daily apprehending that the next post would bring the intelligence that his wife was no more."

At length, however, she also arose from her

sick bed; but arose to grapple, together with her husband, with still deeper sorrows.

A little son had been born to them, who was now about sixteen months old. He was their only and darling child, and was born with such a strange precocity in respect to song that he could sing a tune and beat the time at the age of twelve months. He bore the honored name of *John Wesley*.

As his mother recovered, this sweet child sickened with the same frightful disorder. The father was away in London, attending to the arduous duties of his ministry, and soon receives the sad news touching his little lovely boy. He reads how that he "has the distemper very thick," and that the prospect is dark and uncertain. The fond mother adds that the doctor "is daily here to see our dear Jackey. My heart yearns for him, so that I wish I could bear the distemper again instead of him. But he is in our great Preserver's hands, who cares for him. Farewell!"

His father never looked upon this little boy

again; when he returned, the beautiful form was buried, and the sweet music of his little voice had died away, and the itinerant's home was desolate.

Labeled upon a little neat package, and in elegant letters traced by the bereaved mother's hand, he read:

"My dear Jackey Wesley's hair, who died of small pox on Monday, Jan. 7, 1753–4, aged a year, four months, and seventeen days. I shall go to him, but he never shall return to me."

Then Charles Wesley looked upon his wife, heretofore so beautiful, and lo! a dreary change had gone over her once lovely features. It is said that her most intimate friends did not recognize her by looking upon her countenance, so deep and fatal was the impress which the malady had left of its virulence. She appeared no longer young, but there was a seeming of many years having been all suddenly added to her life.

Will her husband love her now that her beauty is so suddenly and so sadly departed?

If at first she trembled under the influence of such dismal fears, they were soon dismissed to the winds, for her true and good husband was wont to declare, in the tenderness and strength of his affection, that he now admired her more than he had ever done before.

---

## METHODISM AND THE CHURCH.

JOHN and CHARLES WESLEY, up to the time of their conversion, (1738,) were Churchmen "of the straitest sect," and exceeded even the bishops in their high church notions and prejudices.

Also after their conversion they continued strongly attached to the Establishment, and were reluctant to indulge anything that appeared like innovations upon the usages of the Church with which they were connected.

Hence these good men were deeply shocked when, as the result of the great revival which had commenced under their ministry, some of their own sons in the Gospel began to preach, and they resolved at once to silence them.

Thus when the news of Thomas Maxfield's preaching at the Foundry reached John Wesley, he was much offended, and hastened back to London to arrest the evil. His mother, then residing at the Foundry, cautioned him to beware. "John," said she, "you know what my sentiments have been. You cannot suspect me of favoring readily anything of this kind; but take care what you do with respect to that young man, for he is as surely called of God to preach as you are. Examine what have been the fruits of his preaching, and hear for yourself."

John accordingly heard Maxfield preach, and at once yielded his approbation; and when, after several years, he requested the Bishop of Derry to ordain Maxfield, the good bishop complied, and on receiving him for ordination, addressed him, saying: "Sir, I ordain you to assist that good man, John Wesley, that he may not work himself to death."

The case of Maxfield was but a specimen.

Many good men arose, the fruits of the great awakening, men of devout spirit, and whose ministrations were sanctioned by the divine blessing, and the conversion and salvation of multitudes.

"Hence the brothers were not only reconciled to this innovation, but defended it, and rejoiced in it as a means which Christ himself had provided for extending his kingdom in the world; and they were the more satisfied because the preachers and their converts attended the religious services of the Established Church. For a time it was not difficult to preserve this state of things, because the societies and preachers were few in number, and were continually under the eye of the brothers, to whose judgment and authority every one paid the most profound deference."

It is added, however, that serious difficulties at length arose, and the question of separation from the Established Church, and of the administration of the sacrament by the preachers, came to be seriously agitated.

John and Charles Wesley were united against any separation of the Methodists from the Church of England.

Many of their preachers, on the other hand, favored a separate organization, and the administration of the ordinances among themselves, independently of the Church ministers.

It cannot be denied that they had reasons of no small weight for desiring such a change. These reasons may be generally summed up as follows:

While in London and Bristol, the two principal points of Methodism, the Lord's Supper was regularly administered by clergymen, in most other places both the preachers and the societies were expected to attend this ordinance in their several parish churches.

In many instances the clergy who officiated in the parish churches were destitute of piety; and hence doubts arose whether such men, though ordained, were true ministers of Christ.

John Wesley, at Epworth, the parish of his

own father, was repelled from the Lord's table, and assaulted before the whole congregation by the clergyman, who was notoriously drunk at the time.

The doctrine taught in the churches was deemed not only defective but positively erroneous, especially where justification by faith, and the work of the Spirit, were peremptorily denied and opposed.

Several of the clergy, as has been noticed in the preceding pages, were directly concerned in instigating riotous proceedings against the Methodists, whereby their property was destroyed, and their lives endangered. And it was urged that if it were the duty of the sufferers to forgive these injuries, it was too much to expect that they would contentedly receive the memorials of the Saviour's death at the hands of such men. It was urged that "if John Nelson could profitably receive the holy communion from the minister who, by bearing false witness against him, had succeeded in tearing him away from his family and sending him into the army, every one had not John's meekness and strength of mind."

Not a few of the clergy absolutely refused to administer the Lord's Supper to Methodists. "When these people approached the table of the Lord, they were singled out among the communicants, and denied the sacred emblems of their Redeemer's body and blood."

Thus, in many instances, the Methodists "were compelled either to receive the Lord's Supper at the hands of their own preachers, or in the dissenting chapel, or to violate the command of the Lord, who has charged all his disciples to 'eat of this bread, and drink of this cup.'"

These, and the like considerations, failed not to excite much uneasiness among the preachers and societies, and there were much agitation and searchings of heart in various directions.

Among the preachers disaffected toward the Establishment were those who were among the most gifted and pious of the brethren.

There was *Joseph Cownley*, whom John Wesley pronounced one of the best preachers in England.

There were the *Perronets*, sons of the venerable Vicar of Shoreham, both of them men of education and talent, as well as of unquestionable piety.

And there was *Thomas Walsh*, a most remarkable man, an Irishman, and educated for the Romish priesthood; to whom John Wesley bears the following testimony:

"I knew a young man, about twenty years ago, who was so thoroughly acquainted with the Bible that if he was questioned concerning any Hebrew word in the Old, or any Greek word in the New Testament, he would tell, after a little pause, not only how often the one or the other occurred in the Bible, but what it meant in every place. Such a master of biblical knowledge I never saw before, and never expect to see again."

All the above-named preachers, as well as some others, generally "absented themselves from the service of the Established Church, and they occasionally administered the Lord's Supper to the people who were like-minded with themselves, and also to one another."

## PAINFUL SOLICITUDE.

CHARLES WESLEY was a zealous Churchman, and the growing tendency of the Methodist preachers against the Establishment, as noticed in the preceding chapter, greatly distressed and troubled him. He is at first jealous of his brother, having fears that he secretly encouraged the irregular proceedings, though he afterward confesses his suspicions to be unfounded.

His earnestness and spirit in the matter under consideration may be best discerned in a few extracts from his correspondence about this time.

To Rev. Mr. Sellon he writes that his brother believes a separation quite lawful, though not expedient; that the preachers are indefatigable in urging John to go so far that he may not be able to retreat; that Mr. Sellon must be at the ensuing Conference if alive; and that the sound preachers must be qualified for ordination.

Again he writes: "What a pity such spirits should have any influence over my brother! They [certain preachers] are continually urging him to a separation: that is, to pull down all he has built, to put a sword in our enemies' hands to destroy the work, scatter the flock, disgrace himself, and go out like the snuff of a candle. . .

"Charles Perronet, you know, has taken upon him to administer the sacrament for a month together to the preachers and twice to some of the people. Walsh and three others have followed his vile example. The consequence you see with open eyes. O that my brother did so too!"

Again: "There is no danger of my countenancing them, but rather of my opposing them too fiercely. It is a pity a good cause should suffer by a warm advocate. If God gives me meekness, I shall, at the Conference, speak and spare not. . . . . We must know the heart of every preacher, and give them their choice of the Church or the meeting. The wound can no longer be healed slightly; those who are disposed to separate had best do it while we are yet alive."

"These letters," observes Mr. Jackson, "are particularly valuable, not only as exhibiting the state of feeling among the Methodist preachers in those times, but for the light which they shed upon Charles Wesley's character. With the real difficulties of the case he did not attempt to grapple. He does not show how the scruples of such men as Cownley, Walsh, and the Perronets could be removed; nor how the spiritual wants of the societies were to be met in those places where they were repelled from the table of the Lord.

"Such was his impetuosity that he could see nothing in the scruples of these men but pride; and he was resolved to force all the people to an attendance upon their several churches, whatever they might hear there, and though they went with the certainty of being driven from the holy communion.

"Such a course was not suited to the occasion.

The persons concerned were not children, either in years, understanding, or piety. They were rebuked but not convinced, and left to utter their complaints in all directions. To treat them in this manner was only to restrain the evil for a time. It was not removed.

"John Wesley pursued a different course. He also was anxious to preserve the people and preachers in communion with the Established Church, but he would not, even for the attainment of this object, dismiss from the itinerant ministry men of whose uprightness, piety, and usefulness, he had the fullest evidence. Nor would he deal harshly with men whom he thought to be in error, when he saw that conscience was concerned."

With the result of the Conference alluded to Charles Wesley appears to have been but very partially satisfied. The two brothers expressed their minds freely and strongly, and every one was invited to declare his views without restraint.

"Mr. Walsh and his friends engaged to desist

from the administration of the Lord's Supper; such was their deference to the judgment of their brethren, and especially to the Wesleys, who were over them in the Lord.

"With this general conclusion Mr. John Wesley appears to have been satisfied. The practical object which he had in view was gained, and he would not interfere with the workings of private conscience, except in the way of reasoning and persuasion.

"Not so his more ardent brother. Charles perceived that many of the preachers were unconvinced, so that future agitations would in all probability arise, and obstruct the harmony which, for the present, was established. The permanent maintenance of strict Churchmanship he saw to be more than questionable.

"Early, therefore, in the morning of the day after the debate was closed in the conference, he left Leeds, without even informing his brother of his intention, and returned to London."

John Wesley, in writing his brother Charles, endeavors to modify his zeal for outward conformity, and gives him more practical views of their calling. His words are strongly characteristic:

"Do not you understand that they all promised, by Thomas Walsh, not to administer even among themselves? I think that a huge point given up, perhaps more than they could give up with a clear conscience. They showed an excellent spirit in this very thing. Likewise when I (not to say you) spoke once and again with sufficient authority, when I reflected on their answers I admired their spirit and was ashamed of my own.

"The practical conclusion was, not to separate from the Church. Did we not all agree in this? Surely either you or I must have been asleep, or we could not differ so widely in a matter of fact. Here is Charles Perronet raving because his friends have given up all; and Charles Wesley, because they have given up nothing; and I in the midst, staring and wondering both at the one and the other."

A few days afterward John again writes to Charles as follows:

"Wherever I have been in England, the societies are far more firmly and rationally attached to the Church than they ever were before. I have no fear about this matter. I only fear for the preachers' or people's leaving, not the Church, but the love of God, and inward and outward holiness. To this I press them forward continually. I dare not, in conscience, spend my time and strength on externals. If, as my lady says, all outward establishments are Babel, so is this Establishment. Let it stand for me. I neither set it up nor pull it down. But let you and I build up the city of God."

Thus closed up with Charles Wesley the eventful year of 1755. His anxieties were profound and incessant, yet he continued the exercise of his ministry with his wonted energy and success, and his ever active mind poured forth its feelings in sacred verse. Nothing could separate him, either in labor or affection, from his brother, notwithstanding their diversity of opinion in respect to the national Church, and the certain prospect of their future collision on the same subject."

## RETIREMENT.

About 1756, when Charles Wesley was forty-eight years of age, he seems to have mostly ceased his itinerant career. Gradually his journeys became fewer and more limited, until his ministrations were chiefly confined to London and Bristol.

There were, doubtless, several reasons for this which operated with Charles. His marriage, together with an increasing family, may be reckoned as one reason. At first his wife was wont to accompany him extensively in his preaching excursions. Yet this soon became inconvenient, and regard for the feelings and society of his wife, together with the care of his children, very materially contributed to detain him at home.

"Yet the principal cause of his settlement, in all probability, was the state of feeling which existed in many of the societies and preachers with regard to the national Church. He deemed it a matter of absolute duty that they should all remain in strict communion with her.

"His brother thought separation highly inexpedient; but he could not view it in that heinous light in which it appeared to Charles. In reference to this subject he was therefore inclined to moderate counsels, and satisfied himself with gentleness and persuasion in dealing with those who were disaffected toward the Establishment, while Charles was prepared for the adoption of strong and compulsive measures.

"Here was, therefore, an obvious difficulty. Charles could not visit the principal societies in Great Britain and Ireland as a mere friend, or as one of the preachers. He must appear as possessing a co-ordinate authority with his brother; and as their views differed so very materially, they could not, in regulating the affairs of the societies, act in perfect concert.

"Hence, he appears to have thought it the best course for him to retire, and leave the people and preachers generally in the hands of John, whose talents for government were of the highest order. Charles could write hymns with a facility and power which no man of his age could equal; and few could surpass him as an awakening and effective preacher, but he had no aptitude for controlling and harmonizing the discordant spirits of men. For the maintenance of discipline in cases of difficulty, his faculties and habits were not at all suited. His uprightness, generosity, and the kindness of his heart were unquestionable; but his impetuosity created prejudice, and left a soreness in the minds which his brother could easily conciliate and direct.

"Though he ceased to travel, his union with the Methodists remained to the end of his life; and he rendered most important service to the cause of true religion, though in a more limited sphere than he had been accustomed to occupy. He still cultivated his talent for poetry; and the numerous publications which he sent forth into the world possessed a rich and substantial value.

"The societies in London and Bristol were highly favored in retaining the ministrations of such a man. But the loss to the other societies was great, for he usually carried a blessing with him wherever he went. Few men in modern times have more fully exemplified the peculiar characteristics of the eloquent Apollos. He was, indeed, 'fervent in spirit' and mighty in the Scriptures; and by the resistless energy of his preaching he 'mightily convinced' the adversaries of Christ, with formalists and triflers of every description. His power in prayer was equally striking."

It is said, however, that the effect of his retiring from the itineracy was far from being favorable in its influence upon himself. "His mind was naturally inclined to view things in a gloomy and discouraging aspect. But amid the excitement, the change, and the toil of the itinerant ministry, he had no time to be melancholy, however he might be constitutionally disposed to indulge that morbid feeling. The manifest success which attended his preaching filled him with unutterable gratitude, and while all his powers were engaged in his work, he enjoyed a heaven upon earth.

When he ceased to travel he was at leisure to cherish his painful forebodings. Croakers and busybodys tormented him with letters, complaining of the ambition of the preachers, and of the alienation of the people from the Church; and the pernicious leaven of mysticism which he had imbibed at Oxford, and from which his mind had never been thoroughly purged, regained its ascendency over him, so as often to interfere with his spiritual enjoyments. Yet his piety and integrity of purpose were unimpeachable.

"Often was he in agonies of fear lest the Methodists should leave the Church when he and his brother were dead; while John was as happy as an angel, flying through the three kingdoms, sounding the trumpet of the world's jubilee, and joyfully witnessing, every successive year, the steady advancement of the work of God."

About this period John published a pamphlet entitled, "Reasons against a Separation from the Church of England."

These "Reasons" were twelve in number, and were proposed in a spirit the most mild and conciliatory. He introduces the discussion by saying: "Whether it be *lawful* or no, it is by no means *expedient* for us to separate from the Church of England."

Charles, in indorsing this pamphlet, assumes higher ground, and affixed thereto the postscript following: "I think myself bound in duty to add my testimony to my brother's. His twelve reasons against our ever separating from the Church of England are mine also. I subscribe to them with all my heart. Only with regard to the first; I am quite clear that it is neither *expedient* nor *lawful* for me to separate, and I never had the least inclination or temptation so to do. My affection for the Church is as strong as ever, and I clearly see my calling, which is to live and die in her communion. This, therefore, I am determined to do, the Lord being my helper."

## LETTERS.

An occurrence very alarming to Charles Wesley followed soon. It was that Paul Greenwood, John Martin, and Thomas Mitchell, the three preachers stationed at Norwich, overcome by the importunity of some members of the society, had undertaken to administer the sacrament of the Lord's supper. They did this without consulting either of the Wesleys.

Charles immediately addressed a letter to his brother, and several of the older preachers, on the subject.

Some extracts from these letters will evince sufficiently his apprehensions of the calamitous consequences of such a step.

To his brother John he writes thus:

"DEAR BROTHER,—We are come to the Rubicon. Shall we pass, or shall we not? In the fear of God (which we both have) and in the name of Jesus Christ, let us ask, Lord, what wouldest *thou* have us to do?

"The case stands thus: three preachers whom we thought we could have depended upon, have taken upon them to administer the sacrament without any ordination, and without acquainting us (or even yourself) of it beforehand. Why may not all the other preachers do the same if each is judge of his own right to do it? And every one *is* left to act as he pleases, if we take no notice of them that have so despised their brethren.

"That the rest will soon follow their example I believe; because, 1. They think they may do it with impunity. 2. Because a large majority imagine they have a right, as preachers, to administer the sacraments. So long ago as the conference at Leeds, I took down their names. 3. Because they have betrayed an impatience to separate. The preachers in Cornwall, and others, wondered it had not been mentioned at our last conference. . . . .

"Upon the whole, I am fully persuaded almost all our preachers are corrupted already. More and more will give the sacrament and set up for themselves, even before we die; and all, except the few that get orders, will turn Dissenters before or after our deaths.

"You must wink very hard not to see all this. You have connived at it too long. But I now call upon you to consider with me what is to be done, first, to prevent a separation; secondly, to save the few uncorrupted preachers; thirdly, to make the best of those that are corrupted."

To Mr. Nicholas Gilbert Charles writes as follows:

"You have heard of Paul Greenwood, John Murlin, and Thomas Mitchell's presuming to give the sacrament at Norwich. I am the more afflicted thereat because I had as great a love for, and confidence in them, as in any of our sons in the Gospel. They never acquainted their fellow-laborers, no, not even my brother, of their design. They did it without any ordination, either by bishops or elders, upon the sole authority of a sixpenny license; nay, all had not that. Do you think they acted right? If the other preachers follow their example, not only separation, but general confusion must follow.

"I shall tell you my mind plainly, because I love you. My soul abhors the thought of separating from the Church of England. You and all the preachers know, if my brother should ever leave it, I should leave him, or, rather, he me. While ye have any grace remaining ye can never desire to part us whom God hath joined. You would rather waive your right, if you had it, (which I absolutely deny,) of ordaining yourselves priests, than occasion so great an evil.

"Indeed, you must become at last either Church ministers or Dissenters. Such as addict themselves thereto, God will make a way for their regular ordination in the Church. With these I desire to live and die. If you are of the number I look upon you as my brother, my son, and owe you all I can do for you as to soul, body, and estate. I never proposed a friendship and proved false to my profession. I never (that I know) forgot a kindness done me. Your fidelity to the Church of England, although your duty, I shall accept as the greatest kindness you can possibly show me, beyond any personal benefit whatsoever.

"Now consider, and speak your mind. Will you take me for your father, brother, friend? or will you not?"

He writes as follows to John Nelson:

My dear Brother,—I think you are no weathercock. What think you, then, of licensing yourself as a Protestant Dissenter, and baptizing and administering the Lord's supper, and all the while calling yourself a Church of England man? Is this honest? consistent? just? Yet this is the practice of several of our sons in the Gospel, even of some whom I most loved and most depended upon. Who would have thought that Paul Greenwood could be carried away by such dissimulation? He and John Murlin, and Thomas Mitchell, and now, I suppose, Isaac Brown, give the sacrament at Norwich. My brother suffers them. Will not all the rest follow their example? And will not separation, yea, and general separation, ensue? And must not the work of God, so far as we are concerned, be thereby destroyed?

"John, I love thee from my heart; yet rather than see thee a Dissenting minister, I wish to see thee smiling in thy coffin.

"What can be done to save our preachers? Let all things be done in love, and meekness, and the spirit of prayer."

To the Rev. Mr. Grimshaw, a clergyman and a Methodist, he thus writes:

"I am convinced things are come to a crisis. We must now resolve either to separate from the Church, or to continue in it the rest of our days. If pride and the enemy did not precipitate them, our preachers would infallibly find the door into the outward ministry opened to them soon. Such as addict themselves to the service of the Dissenters, we should let depart in peace. Such as dare trust in God, and venture themselves in the same bottom with us, we should cherish them as sons, and do our utmost for them as to soul, body, and estate.

"But this I insist upon, every preacher must know his own mind and his brethren's; must be able to answer, What will become of me after our fathers are gone? Must not I become either a Dissenting or Church minister? Which would I choose?

"To have them and things as they are, is to betray our charge, to undermine the Church, and, as far as in us lies, to destroy the work of God.

"I have read the 'Reasons' to the society here, and their hearts are as the heart of one man. Will you not join hand and heart with us in confirming the souls of the disciples? I anticipate your answer; for I know you pray for the peace of Jerusalem, and you prosper because you love her."

These letters are sufficient. They show where stood the good and zealous Charles Wesley. He seems to have forgotten how far he had himself dissented from the rules of the Church of England, and that he and his brother, with all their attachment to the Church, and resolution never to leave it, were as positive innovators upon its customs as any of the preachers whom they superintended. His shocking declaration to John Nelson, that he would rather see him in his coffin than a Dissenting minister, bespeaks the blinded bigot a hundred fold more than it does the enlightened evangelist.

John Wesley had a loftier and purer vision. He loved the Church, but he loved the conversion of multitudes of souls better; and hence his beautiful sentiment addressed to Charles: "Church or no Church, let you and me build up the city of God!"

Happily for the cause of evangelism, John Wesley was in his full strength in this great crisis, and was enabled to keep a single eye. "The fact is," says Mr. Jackson, "Mr. Charles Wesley was a poet and a preacher; but he had not, as he himself confessed, the practical wisdom which was requisite to superintend and conduct an extensive work of God like that with which he was connected.

"Happily for the Methodists and the world, the preachers had entire confidence in the judgment of his brother, who kept them steadily engaged in the work of saving souls. In the exercise of a noble faith, they persevered in their original calling. They sought not the clerical office for a morsel of bread, and God in his providence took care of their temporal interests."

## LETTERS—CONTINUED.

At this point of time, 1765, we view John Wesley at the age of sixty-two, and Charles at fifty-seven.

The health of Charles is delicate, and his strength is decaying, and he has a solemn impression that his sun of life is rapidly hastening to its setting.

John seems to have thought that Charles had become too much domesticated, and did not sufficiently exert his remaining strength in the great work of God. He accordingly sits down and addresses to Charles the following characteristic letters:

"Dear Brother,—We must, we must, you and I at least, be all devoted to God. Then wives, and sons, and daughters, and everything else, will be real invaluable blessings. 'Come, bestir yourself, and lay aside delay.' Let us this day use all the power we have! If we have enough, well; if not, let us this day expect a fresh supply.

"How long shall we drag on thus heavily, though God hath called us to be chief conductors of such a work? Alas! what conductors! If I am, in some sense, the head and you the heart of the work, may it not be said, 'the whole head is sick, and the whole heart is faint?'

"Come, in the name of God, let us arise and shake ourselves from the dust! Let us strengthen each other's hands in God, and that without delay. Have *senes sexagenarii* [old men of sixty years] any time to lose? Let you and me, and our house, serve the Lord in good earnest. May his peace rest on you and yours! Adieu."

After a few months he addresses Charles again:

"I think you and I have abundantly too little intercourse with each other. Are we not old acquaintance? Have we not known each other for half a century? And are we not jointly engaged in such a work as probably no two other men upon earth are?

"Why, then, do we keep at such a distance? It is a mere device of Satan. But surely we ought not, at this time of day, to be ignorant of his devices. Let us therefore make a full use of the little time that remains. We, at least, should think aloud, and use to the uttermost the light and grace on each bestowed. We should help each other

'Of little life the best to make,
And manage wisely the last stake.'

O insist everywhere on full redemption, receivable now by faith alone! consequently to be looked for now. You are made, as it were, for this very thing. Just here you are in your element. In connection I beat you, but in strong, short, pointed sentences, you beat me. Go on in your own way, what God has peculiarly called you to. Press the instantaneous blessings; then I shall have more time for my peculiar calling, enforcing the gradual work."

Charles is laboring at London, whence he thus writes to his wife at Bristol:

"My work, I very well know, keeps me alive more than it wears me out. That and my life will probably end together. It is superfluous, yet I cannot help cautioning you about Charles, (and Sally too,) to take care he contracts no acquaintance with other boys. Children are corrupters of each other.

"My brother, I presume, will look in upon you on Wednesday se'nnight, in his flight to Land's End. He is an astonishing youth! and may be saluted like the Eastern monarchs: 'O king, live forever!'

"Last night my brother came. This morning we spent two blessed hours with George Whitefield. The threefold cord, we trust, will never more be broken. On Tuesday next my brother is to preach in Lady Huntingdon's chapel at Bath. That and all her chapels (not to say, as I might, herself also) are now put into the hands of us three."

Not long after the above letters were written, Charles Wesley receives from his wife the sad news of the death of an infant boy. He returns the following answer to his sorrowing partner:

"'Father, not as I will, but as thou wilt. Thy will be done on earth, as it is in heaven.'

"Let my dearest companion in trouble offer up this prayer with as much of her heart as she can; and God, who knoweth whereof we are made, and considereth that we are but dust, will, for Christ's sake, accept our weakest, most imperfect desires of resignation. I know the surest way to preserve our children is to trust them with him, who loves them infinitely better than we can do.

"I received your trying news at nine this morning; walked directly with my sympathizing friend F. to take a place. All full but the Bath coach to-morrow morning. I shall come thereby somewhat later to my beloved Sally, and Charley, and his sister. But the Lord is with you already. The Lord is with you always.

This has been a solemn day. You must not deny my love to my sweet boy, if I am enabled to resign him for his heavenly Father to dispose of. I cannot doubt his wisdom or goodness. He will infallibly do what is best, not only for his own children, but for us, in time and eternity. Be comforted by this assurance. Many mourn with and pray for you and your little ones.

"I shall tread on the heels of my letter if the Lord prosper my journey. He comes with me. Let us confidently expect him, the great Physician of soul and body.

"Peace be with you! May the Lord Jesus himself speak it to your heart: 'My peace I give unto you!'"

The above letter is followed soon by another, that tells of his intention to remove his family to London. "Our preparation," he writes, "could not save the first Jackey, because God had prepared a better thing for him. The means may keep Samuel with us. Let us be thankful that he still holds up. If he should have the distemper soon, I believe it will only lessen his beauty. I long to see him and you; but I fear I must be detained another week in town.

"On Monday Mr. Kemp, and Beck, and I go to see a house at Hackney, and another at Newington, either of which, he thinks, will suit us exactly. If Beck and I are of the same judgment we shall take it. . . . My brother himself is quite pleased with our having a house near London; so are all the people, which I need not tell you."

## REMOVAL AND EFFORTS.

IT was in the year 1771 that Charles Wesley changed his residence from Bristol to London.

A lady of fortune, who was a friend of Charles and his wife, handed over to him the lease (which had twenty years to run) of her handsome town residence. The house was richly furnished, and completely prepared for occupancy, and was altogether a most eligible residence, with the exception that it was three miles from the Foundry, the residence of John Wesley when in London.

After his settlement in London Charles served the congregations and societies there with great acceptance and efficiency. He is said to have cherished still that spirit of prayer by which he had ever been distinguished since he had obtained the vital faith in Christ.

There were seasons when he was specially drawn out in prayer for particular friends. Thus, on a Sabbath day in the year 1772, remarking the arduous controversy in which Mr. Fletcher of Madeley was engaged, Charles, with deep feeling, commended that good man to the especial care and blessing of God. He afterward mentioned the subject in a letter to Mr. Fletcher, from whom he received the following remarkable answer: "You asked me in one of your letters how I found myself the Sunday before. [This was the Sunday alluded to.] Your question surprised me so much the more, as I had spent some time that day in wondering how I was inwardly loosed, and how prayer and praise came from a much greater depth than usual in my heart, which, glory be to God! hath, in general, remained with me ever since, together with greater openings of love, and clearer views of Christian simplicity and liberty."

On one occasion, being absent from London during several weeks, he addressed the following interesting and valuable letter to his daughter, who was at school:

"My dear Sally,—Your friends and ours at the Common have laid us under great obligations. I wish I could return them by persuading *her* to seek till she finds the pearl, which is constant happiness; and by persuading *him* to give himself entirely to One whose service is perfect freedom, and whose favor and love is heaven in both worlds.

"I never thought the bands would suit you; yet many of them possess what you are seeking. You also shall bear witness of the power, and peace, and blessedness of heart religion. You also shall know the Lord, if you follow on to know him. Other knowledge is not worth your pains. Useful knowledge, as distinguished from religious, lies in a narrow compass, and may soon be attained if your studies are guarded and directed. We must have a conference on this subject. We may also read your verses together; they want perspicuity, which should be the first point; but they are worth correcting.

"All your powers and faculties are so many talents, of which you are to give an account. You improve your talent of understanding when you exercise it in acquiring important truths. You use your talent of memory aright when you store it with things worth remembering, and enlarge by using and employing it. You should therefore be always getting something by heart. Begin with the first book of Prior's Solomon—The Vanity of Knowledge. Let me see how much of it you can repeat when we meet.

"Miss Hill is likely now to have a good fortune. You need not envy her, if you are a good Christian. 'Seek first the kingdom of God, and all these things shall be added unto you.' Charles has a turn to generosity, Sam. to parsimony. You must balance them both; or you may follow your mother's and my example, and keep in the golden mean.

"There are many useful things which I can teach you if I live a little longer. But I dare never promise myself another year. . . . Probably I have taken my last leave of Bristol. Certainly I shall never more be separated eight weeks from my family. . . . I am nourishing myself up for a journey with my philosophical brother."

Charles Wesley was still as much as ever troubled about the relation of Methodism and the Methodist societies to the Church. He deprecated any separation from the Establishment as one of the greatest calamities.

John Wesley, on the other hand, was less careful in this matter. His vision, as already remarked, was clearer and more extended, and his spirit was more joyous and hopeful. He still persisted, with undiminished zeal, in his career of evangelism, rejoicing with the liveliest gratitude in the prosperity of the work of God. He saw not, as yet, how the societies could be kept together after his death; but he left the whole thing with the Lord, not doubting that he would take care of his own cause.

"Unless the preachers declared themselves to be decided Churchmen, Charles eyed them with alarm. If they were zealous for God, and labored with all their might for the conversion of sinners, John loved them, and encouraged them in their work. He resolved to do what he could to prevent them and the societies from leaving the Church; but their continuance in it was with him a subordinate object. His great concern was to save souls from sin and hell."

## THE FAMILY—CHARLES, JUNIOR.

It is time to notice more particularly the family of Charles Wesley.

We have seen that this marriage was an eminently happy one. His wife proved a true and excellent helpmate, and performed her part with great propriety, and to the full satisfaction of her husband.

Eight children were born to them, of whom five died in their infancy.

John, their first-born, already died of small-pox, 1754, aged sixteen months.

Martha Maria, died 1755, aged one month.

Susanna, named for her honored grandmother, died 1761, aged eleven months.

Selina, named for the Countess of Huntingdon, died 1764, aged five weeks.

John James, died 1768, aged seven months.

"When this fifth death among her children occurred, Mrs. Wesley was deeply distressed, and earnestly besought the Lord, if it were his

LITTLE CHARLEY AT THE PIANO.

will, that she might be spared the pain of following another of them to the grave." Her request was granted, and her other children lived to a good old age. The remaining children were, Charles, born 1757; Sarah, born 1759; and Samuel, born 1766.

Charles Wesley, Junior, seems to have been a musical prodigy. Among the private papers left by his father are the following notices of this child:

"He was two years and three-quarters old when I first observed his strong inclination to music. He then surprised me by playing a tune on the harpsichord readily, and in just time. Soon after he played several, whatever his mother sung, or whatever he heard in the streets. From his birth she used to quiet and amuse him with the harpsichord; but he would not suffer her to play with one hand only, taking the other and putting it to the keys before he could speak. When he played himself, she used to tie him up by his backstring to the chair, for fear of his falling. Whatever tune it was, he always put a true base to it.

"From the beginning he played without study or hesitation, and, as the masters told, perfectly well. Mr. Broadrip, organist at Bristol, heard him in petticoats, and foretold he would one day make a great player. Whenever he was called on to play to a stranger, he would ask, in a word of his own, 'Is he a musicker?' and if answered, 'Yes,' he played with the greatest readiness. He always played with spirit. There was something in his manner above a child, which struck the hearers, learned and unlearned."

"Mr. Rogers, the oldest organist in Bristol, was one of his first friends. He often set him on his knee and made him play to him, declaring he was more delighted in hearing him than himself."

"After hearing him play (at ten years of age) he charged him to have nothing to do with any great master, 'who will utterly spoil you, and destroy anything that is original in you.'"

The lad was placed under the instruction of Mr. Kelway, a most accomplished teacher of music. The following are some of Mr. Kelway's notices of Charles, who was now about twelve years of age:

"I never saw one carry his hand so well. It is quite a picture. It is a gift from God. How would Handel have shaken his sides if he could have heard him!"

"You will be an honor to me. Handel's hands did not lie on the instrument better than yours do."

"Were you my own son I could not love you better. Go on, and mind none of the musicians but Handel. You have a divine gift."

"One cannot hear him play four bars without knowing him to be a genius."

"I will maintain before all the world that there is not a master in London that can play this sonata as he does. The king would eat up this boy. I must carry him some morning to St. James."

"His very soul is harmony. Not one of my

scholars could learn that in a year which he has learned in ten lessons."

"I loved music when young, but not so well as he does. One would think he had been the composer of this. He gives the coloring, the nice touches; the finishing strokes are all his own. I love him better and better. He has it from God. He is a heaven-born child. What coloring! What lights and shades! I could *cry* to hear him.

"He is an old man at the instrument. He is not a boy. He is the greatest genius in music I have ever met with.

"They say I cannot communicate my skill; but I dare maintain there is not such another player as this boy in England, nor yet in France, or Spain, or Italy.

"If I was without the door, and did not know he was dead, I should aver it was Handel himself that played."

Charles enjoyed the advantages of a classical education, but appears to have been incapable of excelling in anything but music, in which he seemed all but inspired. "He was affable, kind, good humored and easy—buried in music—vain of his abilities in the science to which his knowledge was in a great measure limited.

"In his manners he had all the ease and elegance of a courtier; but it is doubtful whether, through the entire course of his life, he was able to dress himself without assistance. If left to himself, he was almost sure to appear with his wig on one side, his waistcoat buttoned awry, or the knot of his cravat opposite one o: his shoulders.

"His morals were correct, and his respect fo: his parents most tender and reverent; but ir early life his mind was not deeply impressed with the solemn truths of religion."

Charles seems to have been a great favorite with the king, George III., who was passionatel fond of Handel's music.

"After the king had lost his sight, Mi Charles Wesley was one day with his majest alone, when the venerable monarch said: 'Mi Wesley, is there any body in the room but yo and me?' 'No, your majesty,' was the reply. The king then said: 'It is my judgment' Mr. Wesley, that your uncle, and your father, and George Whitefield, and Lady Huntingdon have done more to promote true religion in the country than all the dignified clergy put together, who are so apt to despise their labors.'"

An important testimony this; let it be remembered!

## THE FAMILY—SAMUEL.

Samuel Wesley was nine years younger than his brother Charles. His musical genius, as well as that of his older brother, was wonderful. He did not, as a performer, excite so much attention in very early life; yet he surpassed Charles in musical composition. In this latter his precocity was extraordinary.

"The first thing that drew our attention," said his father, "was the great delight he took in hearing his brother play. Whenever Mr.

Kelway came to teach him, Sam constantly attended, and accompanied Charles on the chair. Undaunted by Mr. Kelway's frown, he went on; and even when his back was to the harpsichord, he crossed his hands on the chair, as the other did on the instrument, without ever missing a time." He was between four and five years old when he got hold of the Oratorio of Samson, and by that alone taught himself to read. Soon after he taught himself to write.

"From this time he sprung up like a mushroom, and when turned of five could read perfectly well, and had all the airs, recitatives and choruses of Samson and the Messiah, both words and notes, by heart.

"Before he could write he composed much music. His custom was to lay the words of an Oratorio before him, and sing them all over. Thus he set (extempore for the most part) Ruth, Gideon, Manasses, or the Death of Abel. . . . I have seen him open the Prayer-book, and sing the Te Deum, or an anthem from some psalm, to his own music, accompanying it with the harpsichord.

"Several companies he entertained for hours together with his own music; as quick as his invention suggested, his hand executed it. The learned were astonished. Sir John Hawkins cried out, 'Inspiration! Inspiration!' An old musical gentleman hearing him, could not refrain from tears."

"If he loved anything better than music, it was regularity. Nothing could exceed his punctuality. No company, no persuasion, could keep him up beyond his time. He never could be prevailed on to hear any opera or concert by night. The moment the clock gave warning for eight, away ran Sam, in the midst of his most favorite music. Once he rose up after the first part of the Messiah, with 'Come, mamma, let us go home, or I sha'nt be in bed by eight.' When some talked of carrying him to the queen, and, to try him, asked if he was willing to go, 'Yes, with all my heart,' he answered; 'but I won't stay beyond eight.'

"The praises bestowed so lavishly on him did not seem to affect, much less to hurt him; and whenever he went into the company of his betters, he would much rather have stayed at home. Yet when among them he was free and easy, so that some remarked he behaved as one bred up in a court, yet without a courtier's servility." Indeed, this youth seems to have been everywhere as much admired for his behavior as for his playing.

Yet his character appears to have differed very considerably from that of his brother Charles. "He was possessed of great intellectual power and acuteness. His mind was truly Wesleyan, quick, shrewd, and penetrating. He was mostly educated by his father, especially in Latin. His knowledge was extensive; his conversation elegant, agreeable, instructive, and varied, and he was capable of excelling in any science or profession to which he might apply himself.

"Yet his natural disposition was not so harmless and kindly as that of Charles; nor did he cherish that deep filial affection by which his brother was always distinguished. The father's principal concern respecting Charles was, that he did not give his heart to God. Samuel, even in his youth, showed a waywardness of temper that cost his father many a pang of sorrow."

These two brothers, when grown up, established a series of concerts in their father's house, which were continued through several years, and were attended by many persons of quality.

---

## THE FAMILY—SARAH.

"Miss Sarah Wesley," says Mr. Jackson, "was younger than her brother Charles, and a few years older than Samuel.

"She was born in Bristol, as were all the other children. For some time she attended the school of Miss Temple, in that city; but was taught Latin by her father, as was her brother Samuel also.

"Like both her parents and her brothers, she was little of stature. She bore a striking resemblance to her father in her features, and especially in her profile.

"In mature life she was remarkable for the acuteness and elegance of her mind, as well as for the accuracy and extent of her information, so that she was qualified to move with advantage in the highest literary circles. Miss Hannah More, Miss Benger, Miss Hamilton, Miss Porter, Miss Aikin, Mrs. Barbauld, Dr. Gregory, and many other persons of distinction, were her personal friends, and none of them had any reason to be ashamed of her companionship.

"Her love and esteem for her father were very strong, and his regard for her was tender and enduring. He took great pains in the cultivation of her intellect, and his numerous private letters to her, written when he was separated from his family, show the affectionate interest which he took in her spiritual improvement. It was the intense desire of his heart that she should be a Christian indeed.

"One day, during her childhood, when she was repeating her Latin lesson to him before she had sufficiently mastered it, he said, somewhat impatiently, 'Sarah, you are as stupid as an ass.' She said nothing, but lifted up her eyes with meekness, surprise, and imploring affection. On catching her look, he instantly burst into tears, and finished the sentence by adding, 'and as patient.'

Miss Wesley, possessing the true philosophic spirit, had considerable influence over the mind of her faithful brother Charles. Once when he was somewhat dejected, feeling that his talents had not been adequately rewarded, he came to her, bringing some of his beautiful compositions, and requesting that she would tie them up for him. 'All my works,' said he, 'are neglected. They were performed at Dr. Shepherd's in Windsor, but no one minds them now.'

"She answered in a sprightly tone, 'What a fool you would be to regret such worldly disappointments! You may secure a heavenly crown, and immortal honor, and have a thousand blessings which were denied to poor Otway, Butler, and other bright geniuses. Johnson toiled for daily bread till past fifty. Pray think of your happier fate!'

"'True,' said he, meekly; and took away his productions with sweet humility. Having recorded this anecdote, she adds: 'Lord, sanctify all these mundane mortifications to him and to me! The view of another state will prevent all regrets.'"

We here subjoin a characteristic letter from their uncle John to Sarah and her brother Charles, on the occasion of their wayward brother Samuel's having attached himself to the Roman Church. He commences by alluding to their trouble, because Samuel had changed his religion.

"Nay," he continues, "he has changed his opinion and mode of worship; but that is not religion; it is quite another thing.

"'Has he then,' you may ask, 'sustained no loss by the change?' Yes, unspeakable loss, because his new opinion and mode of worship are so unfavorable to religion that they make it, if not impossible to one who once knew better, yet extremely difficult.

"What, then, is religion? It is happiness in

God, or in the knowledge and love of God. It is faith working by love, producing righteousness, peace, and joy in the Holy Ghost. In other words, it is a heart and life devoted to God; or communion with God the Father and the Son, or the mind which was in Christ Jesus, enabling us to walk as he walked.

"Now either he has this religion or he has not. If he has he will not finally perish, notwithstanding the absurd, unscriptural opinions he has embraced, and the superstitions and idolatrous modes of worship. But these are so many shackles which will greatly retard him in running the race set before him. . . . Therefore you and my dear Sarah have great need to weep over him; but have you not also need to weep for yourselves? For have you given God your hearts? Are you holy in heart? Have you the kingdom of God within you? righteousness, and peace, and joy in the Holy Ghost? the only true religion under heaven.

"O cry unto Him that is mighty to save for this one thing needful. Earnestly and diligently use all the means which God hath put plentifully into your hands! Otherwise, I should not at all wonder if God permit you also to be given up to a strong delusion.

"But whether you were or were not, whether you are Protestants or Papists, neither you nor he can ever enter into glory unless you are now cleansed from all pollution of flesh and spirit, and perfect holiness in the fear of God."

## ASSOCIATES.

From the time that Charles Wesley removed to London he seems to have been honored, notwithstanding his Methodism, with the friendship of several distinguished persons.

"He had free intercourse with Lord Mansfield, whom he had befriended in his boyhood at Westminster school. He sometimes consulted his lordship on questions affecting the Methodists in their relation to the Established Church; and that eminent lawyer declared his readiness to render any service in his power to him and his brother.

Dr. Boyce, one of the fathers of modern Church music, and Mr. Kelway, the musical tutor of Queen Charlotte, were frequent visitors of the family in Chesterfield-street.

"Lord Dartmouth cultivated the friendship of Mr. Charles Wesley on a religious account; and Dr. Johnson mentions him as a person with whose views and habits he was familiar. . . .

"Among Charles's papers are two notes in the hand-writing of the doctor; one addressed to the father, and the other to the daughter, inviting them to dine with him. The first of these is as follows:

"'Sir,—I beg that you, and Mrs. and Miss Wesley, will dine with your brother and Mrs. Hall, at my house in Bolt Court, Fleet-street, to-morrow. That I have not sent sooner, if you knew the discordant state of my health, you would easily forgive me. I am, sir, your most humble servant, Sam. Johnson.'

"'Wednesday.'"

Writing to Miss Wesley, the doctor says:

"MADAM,—I will have the first day that you mention, my dear, on Saturday next; and if you can, bring your aunt with you, to your most humble servant,

"'SAM. JOHNSON.'

"'OCT. 28, 1783.'

"Among Mr. Charles Wesley's friends may also be ranked the late Mr. Wilberforce, then a young statesman just rising into life.

"Their first interview took place at the house of Mrs. Hannah More, and is thus described by that pious and philanthropic man: 'I went, I think, in 1786, to see her, and when I came into the room Charles Wesley rose from the table, around which a numerous party sat at tea, and coming forward to me, gave me solemnly his blessing. I was scarcely ever more affected. Such was the effect of his manner and appearance that it altogether overset me, and I burst into tears, unable to restrain myself.'"

At the same time his early religious associates were soon rapidly disappearing by death.

Thus it was that his tenderest friendships were fast dissolving, and a new generation was rising up around him.

Rev. Henry Piers, the pious vicar of Bexley, died in 1769. He was Charles Wesley's son in the Gospel, shared in the glorious dishonor of early Methodism, a timid and gentle spirit, and was faithful unto death.

Under date of August 24, 1782, John Wesley thus writes: "My brother and I paid our last visit to Lewisham, and spent a few pensive hours with the relict of our good friend, Mr. Blackwell. We took one more walk around the garden and meadow which he took so much pains to improve. Upward of forty years this has been my place of retirement, when I could spare two or three days from London. In that time, first Mrs. Sparrow went to rest, then Mrs. Dewal, then good Mrs. Blackwell, and now Mr. Blackwell himself. Who can tell how soon we may follow them?"

In 1785 died also in great peace Perronet, the excellent vicar of Shoreham, always the fast friend and confidential adviser of the Wesleys.

"When the (Methodist) preachers visited Shoreham, Mr. Perronet's house was their home; and in a room which he fitted up under his own roof, they regularly ministered the word of life. In his spirit and manners he was a perfect gentleman and a Christian, and a more spotless and upright character has seldom adorned any section of the universal Church.

Within three months after the death of Perronet, the great and good Fletcher, another unwavering friend of the Wesleys, passed in triumph from earth to heaven. Few men have ever excelled him in piety, and perhaps no one was ever more honored in death.

"Being indulged with the richest manifestations of God's mercy in Christ, he called upon all around him to unite in the loudest ascriptions of praise. Such was the fullness of his spiritual joy, that he expressed a desire for a gust of praise that should go to the ends of the earth. Having the most elevated and impressive views of the atonement of Christ, he often exclaimed:

> 'Jesus' blood through earth and skies,
> Mercy—free, boundless mercy cries!'

and added, in the full exercise of appropriating faith:

> 'Mercy's full power I soon shall prove,
> Loved with an everlasting love!'

Thus Charles Wesley, now Charles the aged, was entering deeply into that mournful experience of old age, the loss of early friends. One after another they were dropping around him, to be seen on earth no more, and he will soon follow!

## THE WESLEYAN ORDINATIONS.

The flame of Methodism had crossed the Atlantic, and spread itself, to a considerable extent, in this country, while the Wesleys were yet living.

At the close of the war of Independence, and when the great political separation had taken place between England and the American colonies, there was already a membership of about eighteen thousand souls. Several preachers had been sent over by Mr. Wesley, and their labors had been blessed in the conversion of many.

John Wesley deemed it his duty to provide the sacraments as well as the ministry of the word for this increasing multitude. Accordingly, on the morning of September 1, 1784, he, with the assistance of one or two clergymen, solemnly ordained Dr. Coke as superintendent of the American Methodists, with the understanding that the doctor should proceed to America, and ordain Francis Asbury an associate superintendent with himself.

At tho same time Mr. Wesley ordained Messrs. Whatcoat and Vasey as elders for the American work. Also, in the following year, he ordained three preachers to minister the sacraments in Scotland.

"Nothing that Mr. John Wesley ever said or did gave his brother half so much offense as these ordinations. Charles adhered to the principle of 'apostolical succession,' and of the divine appointment of three orders of ministers. Yet he could bear with patience to hear his brother assail these principles in theory, if he only kept the Methodists in union with the Established Church. Whereas he imagined that from these ordinations separation was inevitable.

"The Church of England did not, indeed, exist either in the United States of America or in Scotland; but the principle of presbyterian ordination among the Methodists was recognized; and the men who had received such ordination from his brother, he saw, could, after his brother's death, if not even before, ordain their brethren, and thus introduce the sacraments into the chapels generally, and draw away the societies from their parish churches.

"He had little confidence in Dr. Coke's discretion, and thought that, on his return from America, he might, by possibility, ordain the whole body of the preachers. The elements of separation appeared to him to be now officially adopted and at work; the professions of union with the Church, which he and his brother had reiterated through life, he thought were violated; their strenuous and persevering efforts to resist the spirit of dissent were given up and neutralized, the work of God irreparably injured, and the name of Wesley dishonored forever!

"Such were Charles's extreme views on the occasion, and he mourned that he had not died before the arrival of that day."

About the same time, alluding to his brother John, Charles Wesley writes as follows to a brother clergyman:

"After having continued friends for above seventy years, and fellow-laborers for above fifty, can anything but death part us? I can scarcely yet believe it, that in his eighty-second year, my brother, my old, intimate friend and companion, should have assumed the episcopal character, ordained elders, consecrated a bishop, and sent him to ordain our lay-preachers in

America! I was then in Bristol, at his elbow; yet he never gave me the least hint of his intention. How was he surprised into so rash an action? He certainly persuaded himself that it was right.

"Lord Mansfield told me last year that ordination was separation. This my brother does not, and will not see, or that he has renounced the principles and practices of his whole life; that he has acted contrary to all his declarations, protestations, and writings, robbed his friends of their boasting, and left an indelible blot on his name as long as it shall be remembered.

"Thus our partnership here is dissolved, but not our friendship. I have taken him for better for worse, till death do us part; or rather, reunite us in love inseparable. I have lived on earth a little too long, who have lived to see this evil day. But I shall very soon be taken from it, in steadfast faith that the Lord will maintain his own cause, and carry on his own work, and fulfill his promise to his Church, 'Lo, I am with you alway, even to the end!'"

In a postscript to the same letter Charles prophesies of the "poor Methodists" in America as follows:

"After my brother's death, which is now so near, what will be their end? They will lose all their influence and importance; they will turn aside to vain janglings; they will settle again upon their lees, and, like other sects of Dissenters, come to nothing!"

Events have proved that the good Charles Wesley was more of a poet than a prophet. The "poor Methodists" of America, under the organization established by John Wesley, instead of "coming to nothing," have multiplied so as to be counted by hundreds of thousands, and are the most numerous and the wealthiest Church in the nation.

In reference to the ordinations, he addresses the following earnest letter to his brother:

"DEAR BROTHER,—I have been reading over again your 'Reasons against a Separation,' printed in 1758, and your Works, and entreat you, in the name of God, and for Christ's sake, to read them again yourself with previous prayer, and stop and proceed no further till you have an answer to your inquiry, 'Lord, what wouldst thou have me to do?' Every word of your eleven pages deserves the deepest consideration, not to mention my testimony and hymns. Only the seventh I could wish you to read, a prophecy which I pray may never come to pass.

"Near thirty years since then you have stood against the importunate solicitations of your preachers, who have scarcely at last prevailed. I was your natural ally and faithful friend, and while you continued faithful to yourself, we two could chase a thousand. But when once you began ordaining in America, I knew, and you knew, that your preachers here would never rest till you ordained them. You told me they would separate by and by. The doctor tells us the same. His Methodist Episcopal Church in Baltimore was intended to beget a Methodist Episcopal Church here.

You know he comes armed with your authority to make us all Dissenters. One of your sons assured me that not a preacher in London would refuse orders from the doctor.

"Alas! what trouble are you preparing for yourself, as well as for me and for your oldest, truest, best friends! Before you have quite broken down the bridge, stop and consider! If your sons have no regard for you, have some regard for yourself. Go to your grave in peace; at least suffer me to go first, before this ruin is under your hand.

"So much I think you owe to my father, to my brother, and to me, as to stay till I am taken from the evil. I am on the brink of the grave. Do not push me in, or embitter my last moments. Let us not leave an indelible blot on our memory, but let us leave behind us the name and character of honest men.

"This letter is a debt to our parents, and to our brother, as well as to you, and to your faithful friend."

The following is a part of John's reply:

"All these reasons against a seperation from the Church, in this sense, I subscribe to still. What, then, are you frightened at? I no more separate from it now than I did in the year 1758. I submit still (though sometimes with a doubting conscience) to 'mitered infidels.' I do indeed vary from them in some points of doctrine, and in some points of discipline; (by preaching abroad, for instance, by praying extempore, and by forming societies;) but not a hair's breadth further than I believe to be meet, right, and my bounden duty. I walk still by the same rule I have done for between forty and fifty years. I do nothing rashly. It is not likely I should. The heyday of my blood is over. If you will go on hand in hand with me, do. But do not hinder me if you will not help. Perhaps if you had kept close to me, I might have done better. However, with or without help, I creep on; and as I have been hitherto, so I trust I shall always be, your affectionate friend and brother."

There was other correspondence on the same subject between the brothers, but it ended amicably. "Their love for each other was strong and tender, and if anything could have restrained John from performing his acts of ordination, it was his regard for Charles. But such was his conviction of duty, that he chose rather to grieve the dearest friend he had in the world than refrain from doing that to which he believed himself providentially called in the peculiar exigency of his spiritual children."

## CHARLES WESLEY A POET.

CHARLES WESLEY stood in the first rank as a devotional poet. "In the composition of hymns adapted to Christian worship, he certainly has no equal in the English language, and is perhaps superior to every other uninspired man that ever lived. It does not appear that any person besides himself, in any section of the universal Church, has either written so many hymns, or hymns of such surpassing excellence. Those which he published would occupy about ten ordinary sized duodecimo volumes; and the rest, which he left in manuscript, and evidently designed for publication, would occupy at least ten more. It would be absurd to suppose that all these are of equal value; but, generally speaking, those of them which possess the least merit, bear the impress of his genius."

He was well trained in classical learning, which he cultivated through life. His familiarity with the great poets of antiquity gave him a perfect knowledge of the laws of versification. He possessed at once the true poetic spirit and genius, and the art of poetic expression.

He seems to have written with great ease and freedom, as well as with singular simplicity and variety. "Many of his stanzas are as eloquently free in their construction as even the finest paragraphs of Addison's prose.

"While his sentiments and language are admired by the most competent judges of good writing, his hymns are perfectly intelligible to the common people, thousands of whom, possessed of spiritual religion, feel their breadth and power, and sing them with rapturous delight.

"His meters are very numerous, perhaps more so than those of any other English writer whatever; and it is difficult to say in which of them he most excelled. There are twenty-six meters in the Wesleyan collection in general use, and several others occur in the volumes which Charles published in his own name.

"This variety renders the reading of his books exceedingly agreeable. His cadences never fall on the ear, and never weary the attention. Like scenes in nature, and the best musical compositions, they are perpetually varying, and charm by their novelty."

The same writer adds that "one of the most striking peculiarities of Charles Wesley's poetry is its *energy*. He always writes with vigor, for he is always in earnest. As he felt deeply, and had a singular command of language, he expresses himself with great force. Never does he weaken his lines by unnecessary epithets, or any redundancy of words; and he evidently aimed more at strength than smoothness. Yet he had too fine an ear ever to be rugged; and whenever he chose he could rival the most tuneful of his brethren in the liquid smoothness of his numbers.

"But the crowning excellence of his hymns is the spirit of deep and fervent piety which they everywhere breathe.

"Every feeling of the heart, from the first communication of light to the understanding, producing conviction of sin, and desires after God and Christ, till salvation from sin is attained, the conflicts of the spiritual warfare are ended, and the sanctified believer enters into the heavenly paradise, is embodied in his hymns. The sorrows of penitence, the confidence of faith, the joys of pardon, holiness, and hope; the burning ardor of divine love, the pleasures of obedience, the warmth of universal benevolence, and the anticipations of future glory, he has not merely *described*, but *expressed*, and that in all their fullness and depth. . . .

"The poetical talent that was committed to

the trust of Mr. Charles Wesley involved a responsibility the full extent of which it would be impossible to estimate. He was endued with a power which scarcely any other man has been called upon to wield—a power of promoting the spiritual benefit, not only of the multitudes whom his living voice could reach, but of millions whom he never saw.

"During the last fifty years few collections of hymns, designed for the use of evangelical congregations, whether belonging to the Established Church or the Dissenting bodies, have been made without a considerable number of his compositions, which are admired in proportion as the people are spiritually minded. His hymns are therefore extensively used in secret devotion, in family worship, and in public religous assemblies. Every Sabbath-day myriads of voices are lifted up, and utter, in the hallowed strains which he has supplied, the feelings of penitence, of faith, of grateful love, and joyous hope with which the Holy Ghost, the Lord and Giver of life, has inspired them, and are thus in a course of training for the more perfect worship of heaven.

"Faithfully did he consecrate his talent to the Lord; and the honor which the Lord hath conferred upon his servant is of the highest order, an honor widely extended, and increasing with every successive generation. As long as the language in which they are written is understood, and enlightened piety is cherished, the hymns of this venerable man will be used as a handmaid to devotion. They were not 'obtained by the invocation of Dame Memory and her syren sisters, but by devout prayer to that Eternal Spirit who can enrich with all utterance and knowledge, and sends out his seraphim with the hallowed fire of his altar to purify the lips of whom he pleases.' They are perfectly free from all sickly sentimentality, especially that which modern poets affect, by a perpetual reference to consecrated places, sacred vestments, holy water, and the trumpery of papal Rome, as if religion were a mere matter of the imagination, and Christians were still under the Jewish law. His hymns are as rational and manly in sentiment, as they are pure and elegant in composition. Their theology is thoroughly Scriptural."

## POETICAL SPECIMENS.

We have already, in the preceding pages, inserted a specimen or two of Charles Wesley's poetry. We shall now, as illustrative of statements submitted in the preceding chapter, present a few other specimens.

In the following a lost soul is personated, sinking to ruin in spite of proffered mercy. It is a striking example of the poet's boldness and spirit:

"Hear an incarnate devil preach,
  Nor throw, like me, your souls away,
While heavenly bliss is in your reach,
  And God prolongs your gracious day.

"Whom I reject do you receive;
  The Saviour of mankind embrace;
He tasted death for all; believe,
  Believe, and ye are saved by grace.

"Ye are, and I was once forgiven;
Jesus's doom did mine repeal;
I might with you have come to heaven,
Saved through the grace from which I fell.

"A ransom for my soul was paid;
For mine, and every soul of man,
The Lamb a full atonement made,
The Lamb for me and Judas slain.

"Before I at his bar appear,
Thence into outer darkness thrust,
The Judge of all the earth I clear,
Jesus the merciful, the just.

"By my own hands, not his, I fall;
The hellish doctrine I disprove;
Sinners, his grace is free for all;
Though I am damn'd, yet God is love!"

The two stanzas following are part of a hymn composed upon the road, in behalf of the Irish Roman Catholics:

"If thou wilt work a work of grace,
Who shall the hinderer be?
Shall all the human, hellish race
Detain thy own from thee?
Shall Satan keep, as lawful prize,
A nation in his snare?
Hosts of the living God arise,
And try the force of prayer!

"The prayer of faith hath raised the dead,
The infernal legions driven,
The slaves from Satan's dungeon freed,
And shut and opened heaven.
Our faith shall cleave the triple crown,
Shall o'er the beast prevail;
And turn his kingdom upside down,
And shake the gates of hell."

The beginning of the year 1756 was a dar time in the national affairs of England, and day of public fasting and humiliation was prc claimed by government. It was on this occa sion that Charles Wesley composed the follow ing sublime hymn:

"Stand the omnipotent decree;
Jehovah's will be done;
Nature's end we wait to see,
And hear her final groan.
Let this earth dissolve, and blend
In death the wicked and the just;
Let those ponderous orbs descend,
And grind us into dust;

"Rests secure the righteous man;
At his Redeemer's beck,
Sure to emerge and rise again,
And mount above the wreck.
Lo! the heavenly spirit towers,
Like flames o'er Nature's funeral pyre;

Triumphs in immortal powers,
  And claps his wings of fire.

"Nothing hath the just to lose,
  By worlds on worlds destroy'd;
Far beneath his feet he views,
  With smiles, the flaming void;
Sees this universe renew'd,
  The grand millennial reign begun;
Shouts, with all the sons of God,
  Around the eternal throne.

"Resting in this glorious hope
  To be at last restored,
Yield we now our bodies up
  To earthquake, plague, or sword;
Listening for the call divine,
  The latest trumpet of the seven,
Soon our soul and dust shall join,
  And both fly up to heaven."

In 1759 Charles Wesley published the fourth edition of his "Funeral Hymns."

The following effusion is as energetic and elegant as it is expressive of towering faith and adoring gratitude:

"Merciful God, thyself proclaim,
  In this polluted breast;
Mercy is thy distinguish'd name,
  Which suits a sinner best;

Our misery doth for pity call,
  Our sin implores thy grace;
And thou art merciful to all
  Our lost apostate race.

"Thy causeless, unexhausted love,
  Unmerited and free,
Delights our evil to remove,
  And help our misery.
Thou waitest to be gracious still,
  Thou dost with sinners bear,
That, sav'd, we may thy goodness feel,
  And all thy grace declare.

"Thy goodness and thy truth to me,
  To every soul abound;
A vast unfathomable sea,
  Where all our thoughts are drown'd,
Its streams the whole creation reach,
  So plenteous is the store;
Enough for all, enough for each,
  Enough for evermore.

"Faithful, O Lord, thy mercies are,
  A rock that cannot move;
A thousand promises declare
  Thy constancy of love;
Throughout the universe it reigns,
  Unalterably sure;
And while the truth of God remains,
  The goodness must endure."

The mournful stanzas following were occa-
sioned by the defection of his youngest so

Samuel to Romanism. It is said that of all his sorrows, none had ever touched him so heavily as this. His feelings arose to agony. He regarded his son as lost to him and to the rest of the family, and the very sight of him caused the father's heart to bleed afresh:

"Farewell, my all of earthly hope,
My nature's stay, my age's prop,
Irrevocably gone!
Submissive to the will divine,
I acquiese, and make it mine—
I offer up my son!

"But give I God a sacrifice
That costs me naught? my gushing eyes,
The answer sad express;
My gushing eyes and troubled heart,
Which bleeds with its beloved to part,
Which breaks through fond excess.

"Yet since he from my heart is torn,
Patient, resigned, I calmly mourn
The darling snatched away;
Father, with thee thy own I leave;
Into thy mercy's arms receive,
And keep him to that day.

"Keep, for I nothing else desire,
The bush unburn'd amid the fire,
And freely I resign

My child, for a few moments lent,
(*My child no longer!*) I consent
To see his face no more!

"But hear my agonizing prayer,
And O, preserve him, and prepare
To meet me in the skies,
When throned in bliss the Lamb appears,
Repairs my loss and wipes the tears
Forever from my eyes!"

The following hymn, "Wrestling Jacob," is the one which Dr. Watts considered "worth more than all the verses he had written:"

"Come, O thou traveler unknown,
Whom still I hold, but cannot see;
My company before is gone,
And I am left alone with thee:
With thee all night I mean to stay,
And wrestle till the break of day.

"I need not tell thee who I am;
My sin and misery declare;
Thyself hast call'd me by my name;
Look on thy hands, and read it there.
But who, I ask thee, who art thou?
Tell me thy name, and tell me now.

"In vain thou strugglest to get free;
I never will unloose my hold:
Art thou the man that died for me?
The secret of thy love unfold:
Wrestling, I will not let thee go,
Till I thy name, thy nature know.

"Wilt thou not yet to me reveal
  Thy new, unutterable name?
Tell me, I still beseech thee, tell;
  To know it now resolved I am:
Wrestling, I will not let thee go,
Till I thy name, thy nature know.

"What though my shrinking flesh complain,
  And murmur to contend so long?
I rise superior to my pain:
  When I am weak, then I am strong:
And when my all of strength shall fail,
I shall with the God-man prevail.

"Yield to me now, for I am weak,
  But confident in self-despair;
Speak to my heart, in blessings speak;
  Be conquer'd by my instant prayer:
Speak, or thou never hence shalt move,
And tell me if thy name be Love.

"'Tis Love! 'tis Love! thou diedst for me;
  I hear thy whisper in my heart;
The morning breaks, the shadows flee;
  Pure, universal Love thou art:
To me, to all, thy bowels move;
Thy nature and thy name is Love.

"My prayer hath power with God; the grace
  Unspeakable I now receive;
Through faith I see thee face to face;
  I see thee face to face, and live!
In vain I have not wept and strove;
Thy nature and thy name is Love.

"I know thee, Saviour, who thou art—
  Jesus, the feeble sinner's Friend:
Nor wilt thou with the night depart,
  But stay and love me to the end:
Thy mercies never shall remove;
Thy nature and thy name is Love.

"The Sun of righteousness on me
  Hath risen with healing in his wings:
Wither'd my nature's strength, from thee
  My soul its life and succor brings:
My help is all laid up above;
Thy nature and thy name is Love.

"Contented now, upon my thigh
  I halt, till life's short journey end;
All helplessness, all weakness, I
  On thee alone for strength depend;
Nor have I power from thee to move;
Thy nature and thy name is Love.

"Lame as I am, I take the prey;
  Hell, earth, and sin, with ease o'ercome;
I leap for joy, pursue my way,
  And, as a bounding hart, fly home,
Through all eternity to prove
Thy nature and thy name is Love!"

## PREACHING AND SCHOLARSHIP.

Charles Wesley excelled as a preacher, not so much in the *greatness*, as in the *efficiency* of his preaching.

"There was nothing artificial in his sermons. To a strictly logical arrangement, and the arts of secular oratory, he was indifferent. His discourses were the effusions of the heart, rather than the offspring of the intellect, or of the imagination. They were not characterized by abstract reasoning or by showy ornament.

"Of the Bible he was a diligent and enraptured student; and its facts, doctrines, language, and imagery were indelibly engraven upon his mind.

"In the delivery of God's word he expected and received the promised aid of the Holy Spirit, and under the divine unction he spoke with irresistible power and authority.

"His heart was inflamed with zeal for the honor of Christ, and yearned over the souls of the people; the tears ran down his cheeks, his tongue was loosed, and he poured forth the truth of God in the very phraseology of inspiration, with an effect that was overwhelming.

"He gave such views of the evil of sin, and of the certain damnation of the impenitent and unregenerate, as terrified the consciences of the ungodly and the sinner, who fell down upon their knees, and in bitter anguish called upon God for his mercy.

"At the same time he expatiated upon the perfect sacrifice of Christ, the efficacy of his blood, the tenderness of his compassion, and the freeness of his grace, with such a power of conviction as to induce those whose spirits were contrite *even then* to believe to the saving of their souls. He generally delivered his message in short, pointed sentences, which all could understand, and all could feel.

"When his own heart was deeply impressed, he not unfrequently extended his sermon to the length of two hours, and even more; for he felt that he had a work to accomplish—the people were ignorant and wicked, they needed instruction, conversion, salvation. To turn them from sin to Christ was the very end of his preaching; and he knew not how to close the service and dismiss the poor, guilty souls around him until this great design of the divine mercy was fulfilled.

"Often was his heart gladdened by success. Under his ministry many a hardened sinner began to pray; and from the religious services which he conducted, even in the open air, many a penitent publican went to his house justified.

"In the latter years of his life he was so enfeebled by age, disease, and sorrow, that his preaching was rather deliberate and tender, than powerful and awakening. Yet, on some occasions, to the end of his life, it partook of the vehemence and energy which characterized it in his earlier years."

We have the following particular account of his preaching in his last days:

"If his thoughts did not flow freely in the

pulpit he was very deliberate, making long pauses, as if waiting for the promised communication of divine influence. In such cases he usually preached with his eyes closed; he fumbled with his hands about his breast, leaned with his elbows upon the Bible, and his whole body was in motion.

"He was often so feeble as to be under a necessity of once or twice calling upon the congregation to sing, in the course of his sermon, that he might partially recover himself, and be able to finish his discourse. When he had strength, and his mind was under peculiar excitement, as it often was, he expressed himself with fluency and power.

"His sentences were short and pointed, charged with the most weighty truths, and the language was such as all understood and felt. His sermons were the effusions of a heart overflowing with divine truth and love. They were rich in Scripture sentiment and in Scripture phraseology, 'as it were a paved work of sapphire.'

"In prayer he was copious and mighty, especially upon sacramental occasions, when he seemed to 'enter into the holiest of all by the blood of Jesus.'

"Greatly was he enfeebled by age and disease; yet he continued his public religious services, in this spirit and manner, till within a few months of his death."

We have the following notice of his scholarship: "His attainments as a scholar were worthy of the advantages which he enjoyed, as a pupil of Westminster school, and a member of the university of Oxford. With the Latin, Greek, Hebrew, and French languages he was well acquainted. His son Samuel believed that he read German; but his daughter, when questioned on the subject, spoke doubtingly. In a letter addressed to him at Oxford by his father, he is urged to persevere in the study of Arabic, and of the mathematics; but it is probable that, after he left the university, he paid little attention to either of these branches of learning. Classical and Biblical literature he cultivated to the end of his protracted life. His exact and critical knowledge of the Holy Scriptures is strikingly manifest in his hymns. Among the Romans, Horace and Virgil were his favorite authors. Large portions of the Æneid he had committed to memory, and occasionally repeated them, with unrivaled taste and spirit, for the gratification of his friends."

"Considering his scholarship, taste, and genius, there can be no doubt that, had he devoted himself to secular literature, he would have taken a high rank among the poets of Great Britain. He would have rivaled Dryden himself, whom he greatly resembles in fluency, copiousness, and power."

Like his brother John, Charles Wesley was small of stature. He was short-sighted, abrupt and singular in his manners, so that when at college John is said to have dreaded his visits. "He would run against his brother's table, disarrange his papers, ask several questions in quick succession, and often retire without even waiting for answers."

## SOCIAL CHARACTER.

Charles Wesley was eminently a social being, and his soul was formed for friendship. "He possessed such a frankness of disposition, combined with such warmth of affection and integrity of purpose, as at once commanded the esteem and love of all who were likeminded. His sympathies were deep and tender, so that his friendship was felt to be of inestimable value, especially in seasons of affliction, when help is most needed. He was, indeed, a brother born for the benefit of those who are in adversity, and possessed great power to soothe and cheer. The pain and sickness in which much of his life was spent, the successive deaths of five children, added to the natural and gracious tenderness of his heart, enabled him so to enter into the views and feelings of the sorrowful, that they were at once strengthened and encouraged, and blessed God for the consolation of which he made his servant the instrument."

He ever maintained an inviolable friendship for his brother John. As already noticed, he was deeply grieved with some of his brother's acts, and widely differed from him in some of his views; yet his warm affection and friendship never declined. If he sometimes, himself, censured John, he would allow no one else to do it.

"Lady Huntingdon attempted to alienate him from his brother, by telling him, in a private letter, that John was a teacher of 'heresy' and 'popery.' But deeply as he was indebted to her kindness, he rebuked her for her unseemly bigotry, and declared that death itself should never separate him from the brother of his heart. He was linked to him by no selfish feeling, or mere instinct of nature, but by the 'love that never faileth;' and his generous friendship was returned by his brother with equal fidelity and warmth.

"In the various domestic relations the conduct of Charles Wesley was most exemplary. His filial reverence and affection toward both his parents, were as profound as they were justly merited. Toward both his brothers, and all his sisters, he was an example of fraternal kindness. They witnessed through life his readiness to serve them as much as lay in his power.

"What he was as a husband the preceding narrative declares. To his wife he disclosed the secrets of his heart with perfect confidence and unreserve; and in her society he sought for solace when troubled with the affairs of the world and the Church. His concern for her comfort, his sympathy with her in affliction, and, above all, his pious solicitude for her spiritual improvement, are attested in the whole of his correspondence with her, of which many specimens have been given.

Several of his hymns were originally written for her use and benefit. They were acts of supplication in times of necessity and sorrow, of resignation under bereavements, or of adoring gratitude for divine mercies. He received her as a gift from God; he regarded her as his best earthly friend; and he ever treated her as an heir with himself of eternal life.

"Often did he remind her that the most important end of their union was their mutual improvement in personal holiness; and most assiduously did he labor to bring her into increasing union with Christ their living head.

"In a letter which he addressed to her when he felt his strength decay, he says: 'My best of friends,—I am going the way of all the earth; and what shall I do for you before we part? I can only pray, and very imperfectly, that the providential end of our meeting may be answered upon you in both worlds. You married me that you might be holier and happier to all eternity. If you have received less spiritual good than you expected, it is chiefly my fault. I have not set you the pattern I ought. For the same reason I have been of so little use to my children. But it is too late to attempt it now; my night cometh, or rather is come. I leave you to the God of all grace, who is ready to supply all your wants. Time fails me for the rest. I may have another opportunity, I may not. The Lord be yours and your children's portion!'

"Such were the humbling views which this Christian husband and parent entertained concerning himself!"

"His children were mostly educated by himself; and the letters which he addressed to them when they were from home, many of which have been preserved, express the tenderness of his love, and his yearning desire for their salvation."

---

## DEATH.

In the month of February, 1788, commenced the last sickness of Charles Wesley. He was then reduced to great weakness, though still able to go abroad occasionally.

On the 18th of this month he received such a letter as the following from his brother John:

"Dear Brother,—You must go out every day or die. Do not die to save charges; you certainly need not want anything as long as I live."

Shortly after this, John left London on an itinerating excursion, and saw his brother no more. He seems not to have suspected that Charles was so near to die; but strongly looked for him to rally, and still labor in the Gospel.

"The decree, however, was gone forth, and no means could avail for the preservation of his life. While he remained in the state of extreme feebleness to which the letter of John refers, having been silent and quiet for some time, he called Mrs. Wesley to him, and requested her to write the following lines at his dictation:

'In age and feebleness extreme,
Who shall a sinful worm redeem?
Jesus, my only hope thou art,
Strength of my failing flesh and heart;
O could I catch a smile from thee,
And drop into eternity!'

"For fifty years Christ as the Redeemer of men had been the subject of his effective ministry and of his loftiest songs, and he may be said to have died with a hymn to Christ upon his lips. He lingered till the 29th of March, 1788, when he yielded up his spirit into the hands of his God and Saviour, at the advanced age of seventy-nine years and three months."

On the same day, Miss Sarah Wesley addressed her Uncle John as follows:

"Dear and Honored Uncle,—We were all present when my dear respected father departed this life. His end was, what he particularly wished it might be, peace! For some months past he seemed totally detached from earth. He spoke very little, nor wished to hear anything read but the Scriptures. He took a solemn leave of all his friends. I once asked if he had any presages that he should die. He said, 'No;' but his weakness was such that he thought it impossible he 'should live through March.' He kindly bade me remember him, and seemed to have no doubt but I should meet him in heaven.

"All his prayer was, 'patience, and an easy death!' He bade every one who visited him to supplicate for these; often repeating, 'an easy death!' He told my mother, the week before he departed, that no fiend was permitted to approach him; and said to us all, 'I have *a good hope!*' When we asked if he wanted anything, he frequently answered, 'Nothing but Christ!' Some person observed that the valley of the shadow of death was hard to be passed. 'Not with Christ,' replied he.

"On March 27th, after a most uneasy night, he prayed, as in an agony, that he might not have many such nights. 'O my God,' said he, '*not many!*' It was with great difficulty he seemed to speak. About ten days before, on my brother Samuel's entering the room, he took hold of his hand, and pronounced, with a voice of faith, 'I shall bless God to all eternity that ever you were born. I am persuaded I shall!' My brother Charles also seemed much upon his mind. 'That dear boy!' said he, 'God bless him!' He spoke less to me than to the rest, which has since given me some pain. However, he bade me trust in God, and never forsake him; and then he assured me that he never would forsake me.

"The 28th, my mother asked if he had any thing to say to us. Raising his eyes, he said, 'Only thanks! love! blessing!'

"Tuesday and Wednesday he was not entirely sensible. He slept much, without refreshment, and had the restlessness of death for, I think, the whole week. He was eager to depart; and if we moved him, or spoke to him, he answered, 'Let me die! let me die!' A fortnight before he prayed, with many tears, for all his enemies, naming Miss Freeman. 'I beseech thee, O Lord, by thine agony and bloody sweat,' said he, 'that she may never feel the pangs of eternal death.' When your kind letter to my brother came, (in which you affectionately tell him that you will be a father to him and my brother Samuel,) I read it to our father. 'He will *be kind to you*,' said he, 'when I am gone. I am certain your uncle *will be kind* to all of you.'

"The last morning, which was the 29th of March, being unable to speak, my mother entreated him to press her hand if he knew her, which he feebly did. His last words which I could hear were, 'Lord—my heart—my God!' He then drew his breath short, and the last so gently, that we knew not exactly the moment in which his happy spirit fled. His dear hand was in mine for five minutes before, and at the awful period of his dissolution. It had often been his desire that we should attend him to the grave; and though he did not mention it again (which he did the place of his burial) during his illness, we all mean to fulfill his wish, trusting we shall be supported, as we have been hitherto, in our afflicting situations.

"My dear, honored uncle, my mother presents you her respectful love, and my brothers join with me in duty, begging your prayers for the widow and the fatherless! I am your afflicted and dutiful niece."

John Wesley replied to his niece as follows:

"My dear Sally,—I thank you for the account you have given me. It is full and satisfactory. You describe a very awful scene. The time, I doubt not, was prolonged on purpose that it might make the deeper impression on those that might otherwise soon have forgotten it. What a difference does one moment make when the soul springs out of time into eternity! What an amazing change! What are all the pleasures, the business of this world, to a disembodied spirit? Let *us* therefore be ready, for the day is at hand! But the comfort is, it cannot part you long from, dear Sally, yours invariably."

On Saturday, April 5th, Charles Wesley was buried, according to his desire, in the churchyard of St. Mary-le-bone, near his residence. The pall was supported by eight clergymen of the Church of England. On the following day his funeral sermon was preached "in West-street, at the new chapel, to an inconceivable concourse of people, of every description, from 2 Sam. iii, 38: 'A prince and a great man is fallen this day in Israel.'"

On a neat marble tablet in City Road Chapel, London, is inscribed the following epitaph:

"God buries his workmen, but carries on his work."

Sacred to the Memory

OF

THE REV. CHARLES WESLEY, A.M.,

Educated at Westminster School,
and some time Student at Christ Church, Oxford.
As a Preacher,
he was eminent for ability, zeal, and usefulness,
being learned without pride,
and pious without ostentation;
to the sincere, diffident Christian,
a son of consolation;
but to the vain boaster, the hypocrite, and profane,
a son of thunder.

He was the first who received the name of Methodist;
and, uniting with his brother, the Rev. JOHN WESLEY,
in the plan of itinerant preaching,
endured hardships, persecution, and disgrace,
as a good soldier of Jesus Christ;
contributing largely, by the usefulness of his labors,
to the first formation of the Methodist Societies
in these kingdoms.

As a Christian Poet he stood unrivaled;
and his Hymns will convey instruction and consolation
to the faithful in Christ Jesus
as long as the English language is understood.

He was born the xviii of December, MDCCVIII,
and died the xxix of March, MDCCLXXXVIII,
a firm and pious believer in the doctrines of the Gospel,
and a sincere friend to the Church of England.

It only remains that we add the following record:

*Mrs. Wesley*, having survived her husband about thirty-four years, died December 28, 1822, at the advanced age of ninety-six.

*Sarah* died at Bristol, when on a visit to that city, on the 19th of September, 1828, aged sixty-eight years.

*Charles* died in London, May 23, 1834, in the seventy-seventh year of his age.

*Samuel*, also, died in London on the 11th of October, 1837, in the seventy-second year of his age.

Charles and Sarah were never married. They were both members of the Methodist Society. Samuel left several children, who are now living.

THE END.